Disney · PIXAR

COCO

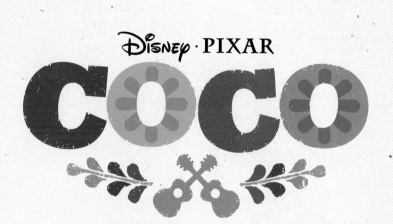

The Story of the Movie in Comics

SCRIPT ADAPTATION
Jai Nitz

ARTIST
Tony Sandoval

COLOR ARTISTS
Alesia Barsukova, Alberto Madrigal,
Liudmila Steblianko, Grzegorz
Krysinski,
Ekaterina Myshalova, Pinchuk Yulia
Leonidovna, Glazytina Tatiana,
Luca Pisanu

LETTERER / GRAPHIC DESIGN
Chris Dickey

COVER ARTIST
Tony Sandoval

DISNEY PUBLISHING WORLDWIDE
Global Magazines, Comics
and Partworks

PUBLISHER
Lynn Waggoner

EXECUTIVE EDITOR
Stefano Ambrosio

EDITORIAL TEAM
Bianca Coletti (Director, Magazines),
Guido Frazzini (Director, Comics),
Carlotta Quattrocolo (Executive Editor),
Camilla Vedove (Senior Manager,
Editorial Development),
Behnoosh Khalili (Senior Editor),
Julie Dorris (Senior Editor)

DESIGN
Enrico Soave (Senior Designer)

ART
Ken Shue (VP, Global Art),
Roberto Santillo (Creative Director),
Marco Ghiglione (Creative Manager),
Stefano Attardi (Computer Art Designer),
Manny Mederos (Comics & Magazines
Creative Manager)

PORTFOLIO MANAGEMENT
Olivia Ciancarelli (Director)

BUSINESS & MARKETING
Mariantonietta Galla
(Marketing Manager),
Virpi Korhonen (Editorial Manager)

CONTRIBUTORS
Alessandro Ferrari, Mina Riazi,
Jonathan Manning

SPECIAL THANKS
Adrian Molina, Scott Tilley

Published simultaneously in the United
States and Canada by Joe Books Ltd,
489 College Street, Suite 203,
Toronto, ON M6G 1A5.

www.joebooks.com

First Joe Books edition: November 2017

Print ISBN: 978-1-77275-531-2

Library and Archives Canada Cataloguing
in Publication information is available upon
request.

Printed and bound in Canada
1 3 5 7 9 10 8 6 4 2

Disney · PIXAR
COCO

JOE BOOKS

IN THE LAND OF THE LIVING...

MIGUEL

is a twelve-year-old boy with a passion for music. Miguel dreams of following in the footsteps of Ernesto de la Cruz—the greatest musician of all time—but he must keep his aspirations hidden from his family, who banned music generations ago. When a magical mishap takes Miguel on an unexpected journey through the Land of the Dead, he meets his ancestors and discovers a thing or two about his past...

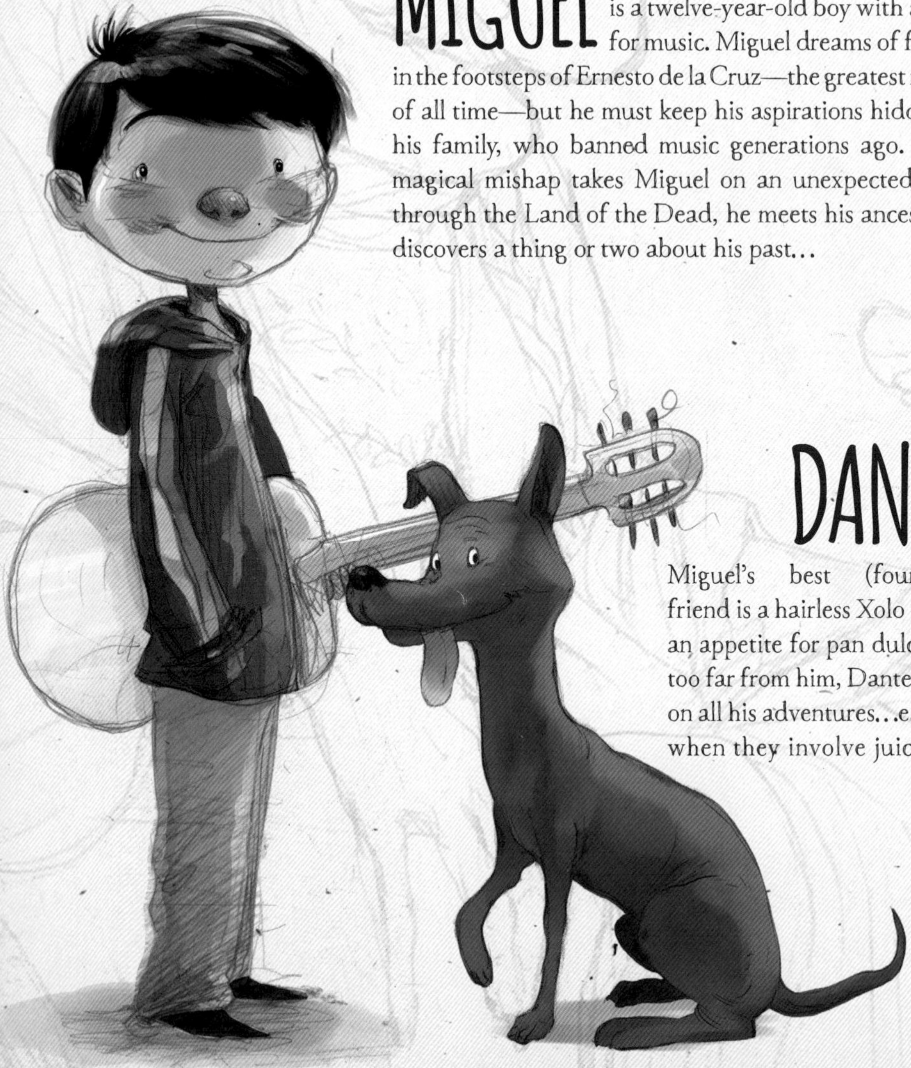

DANTE

Miguel's best (four-legged) friend is a hairless Xolo dog with an appetite for pan dulce. Never too far from him, Dante Miguel on all his adventures...especially when they involve juicy bones!

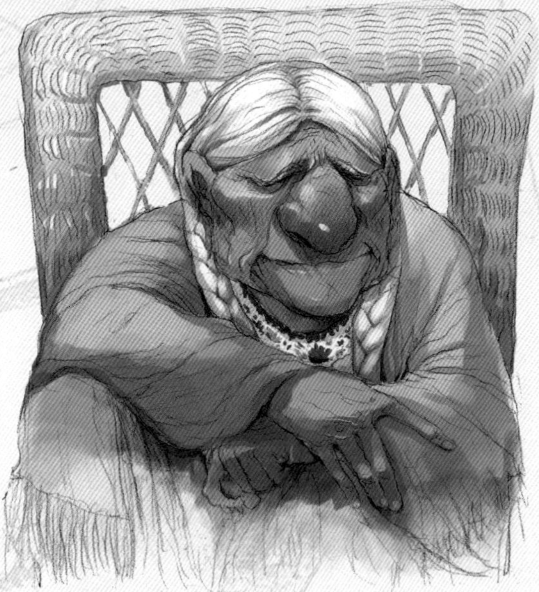

MAMÁ COCO

Miguel's great-grandmother Mamá Coco learned shoemaking from her mother, Mamá Imelda, and always followed the family's number-one rule—no music! Now that she's in her nineties, Mamá Coco has trouble remembering things and spends most of her days in her wicker wheelchair. Miguel loves Mamá Coco and knows she is a good listener—even though she sometimes calls him Julio!

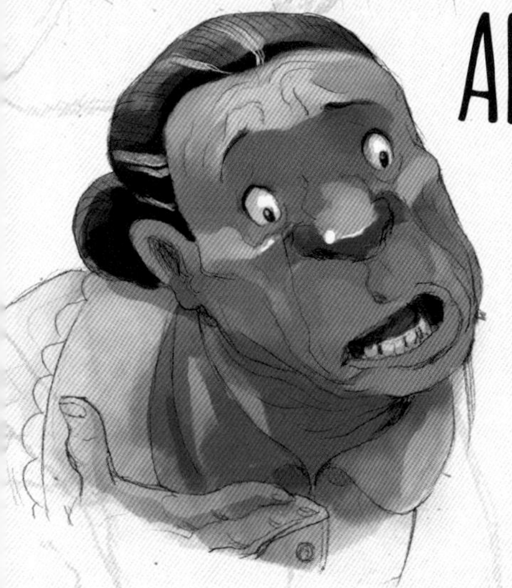

ABUELITA

is Miguel's grandmother and Mamá Coco's daughter. Abuelita is the matriarch of the Rivera household. She strictly enforces the family's most important rule, making sure there's no music in the house—or anywhere near it! Abuelita considers Día de los Muertos an important tradition that brings the family closer.

MAMÁ AND PAPÁ

Like the rest of the Rivera family, Mamá Luisa and Papá Enrique work tirelessly in the family shoe shop, continuing a generations-long tradition they can't wait to pass down to their son Miguel.

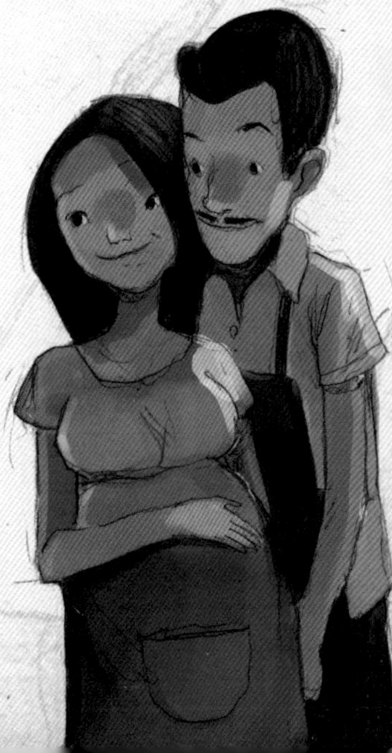

IN THE LAND OF THE DEAD...

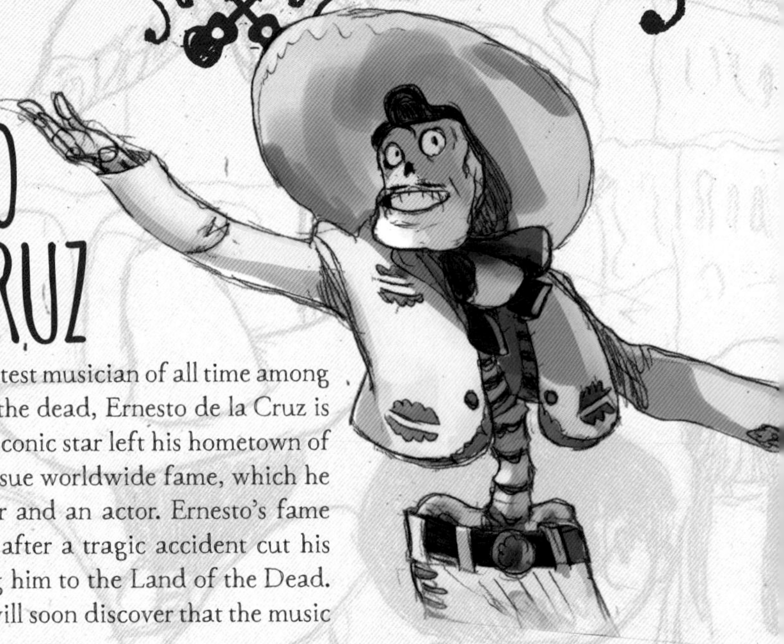

ERNESTO DE LA CRUZ

Considered the greatest musician of all time among both the living and the dead, Ernesto de la Cruz is Miguel's hero. The iconic star left his hometown of Santa Cecilia to pursue worldwide fame, which he achieved as a singer and an actor. Ernesto's fame did not falter even after a tragic accident cut his life short, relocating him to the Land of the Dead. But Ernesto's fans will soon discover that the music legend is not what he seems...

HÉCTOR

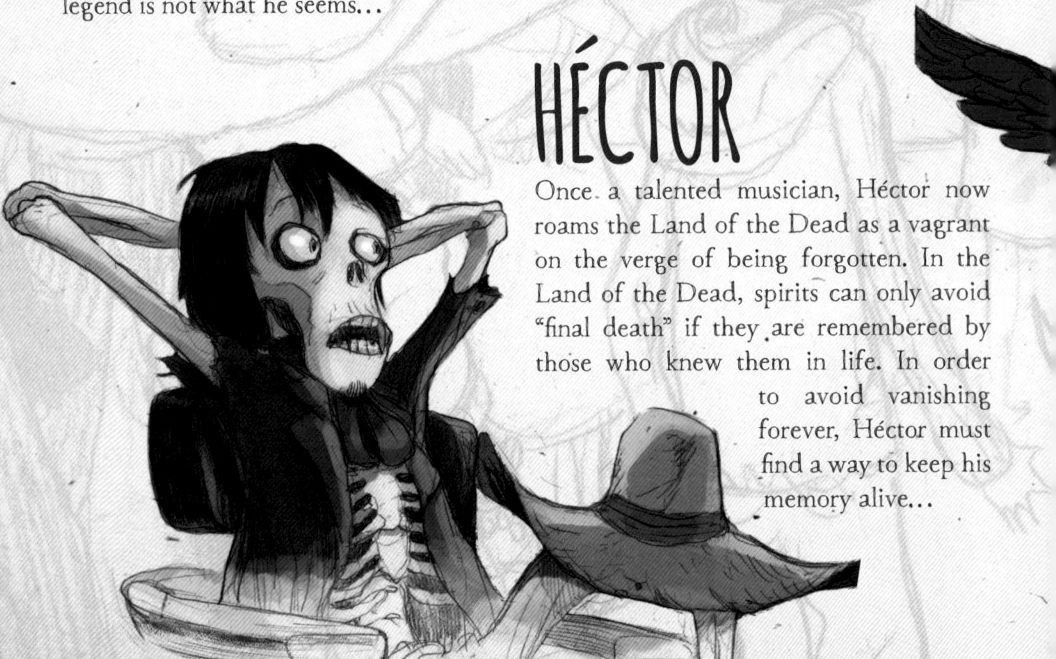

Once a talented musician, Héctor now roams the Land of the Dead as a vagrant on the verge of being forgotten. In the Land of the Dead, spirits can only avoid "final death" if they are remembered by those who knew them in life. In order to avoid vanishing forever, Héctor must find a way to keep his memory alive...

MAMÁ IMELDA

Miguel's great-great-grandmother Mamá Imelda banished music from the Rivera household after her husband abandoned the family to pursue musical stardom. But rather than shed a tear, Mamá Imelda started the Rivera family shoemaking business to provide for her daughter, Coco. Not one to sugarcoat her words, Mamá Imelda firmly opposes Miguel's dreams of becoming a musician.

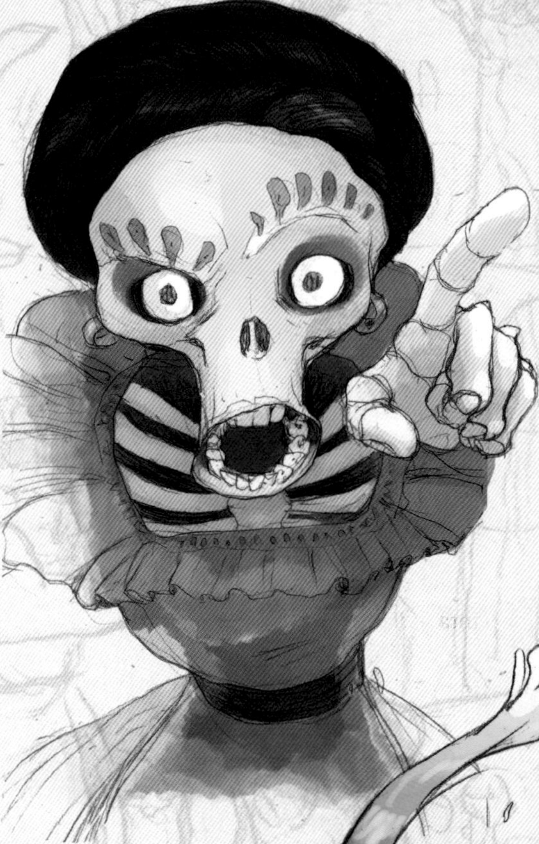

PEPITA

is an alebrije that resembles a jaguar with wings. Pepita is Mamá Imelda's trusty spirit guide. Pepita is the only one who can help Mamá Imelda find her great-great-grandson Miguel and return him to the Land of the Living.

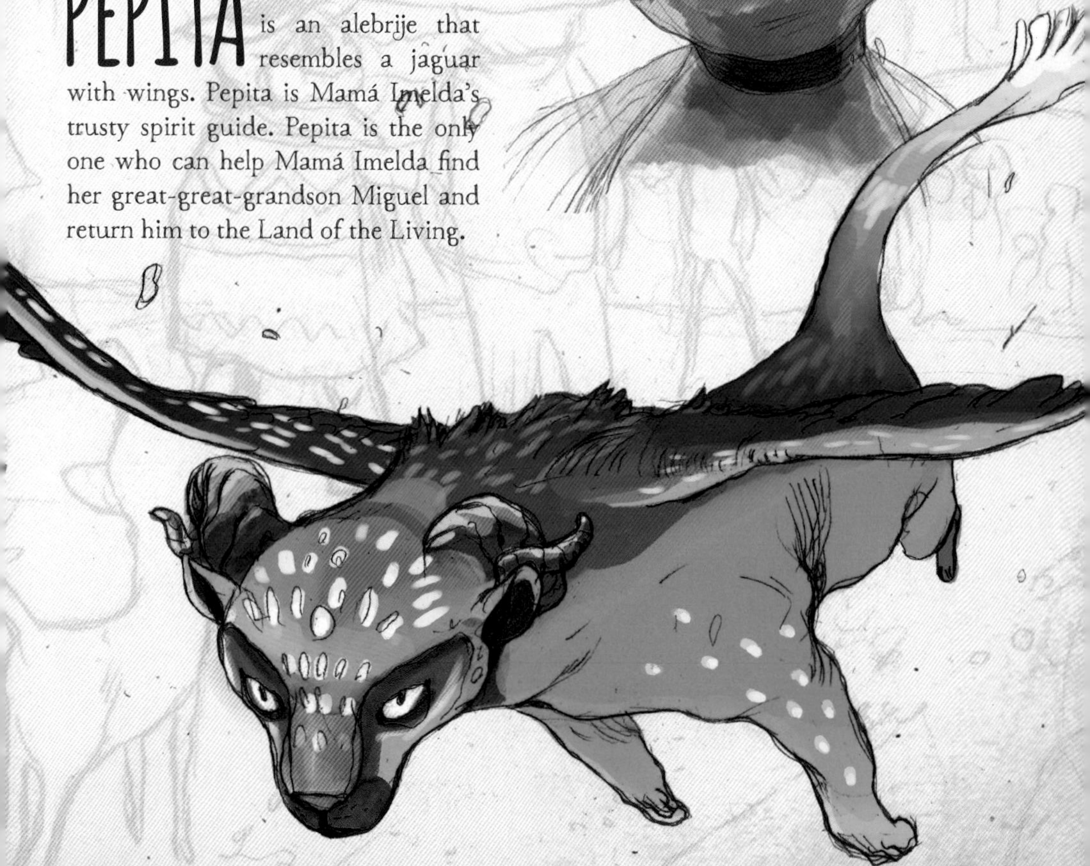

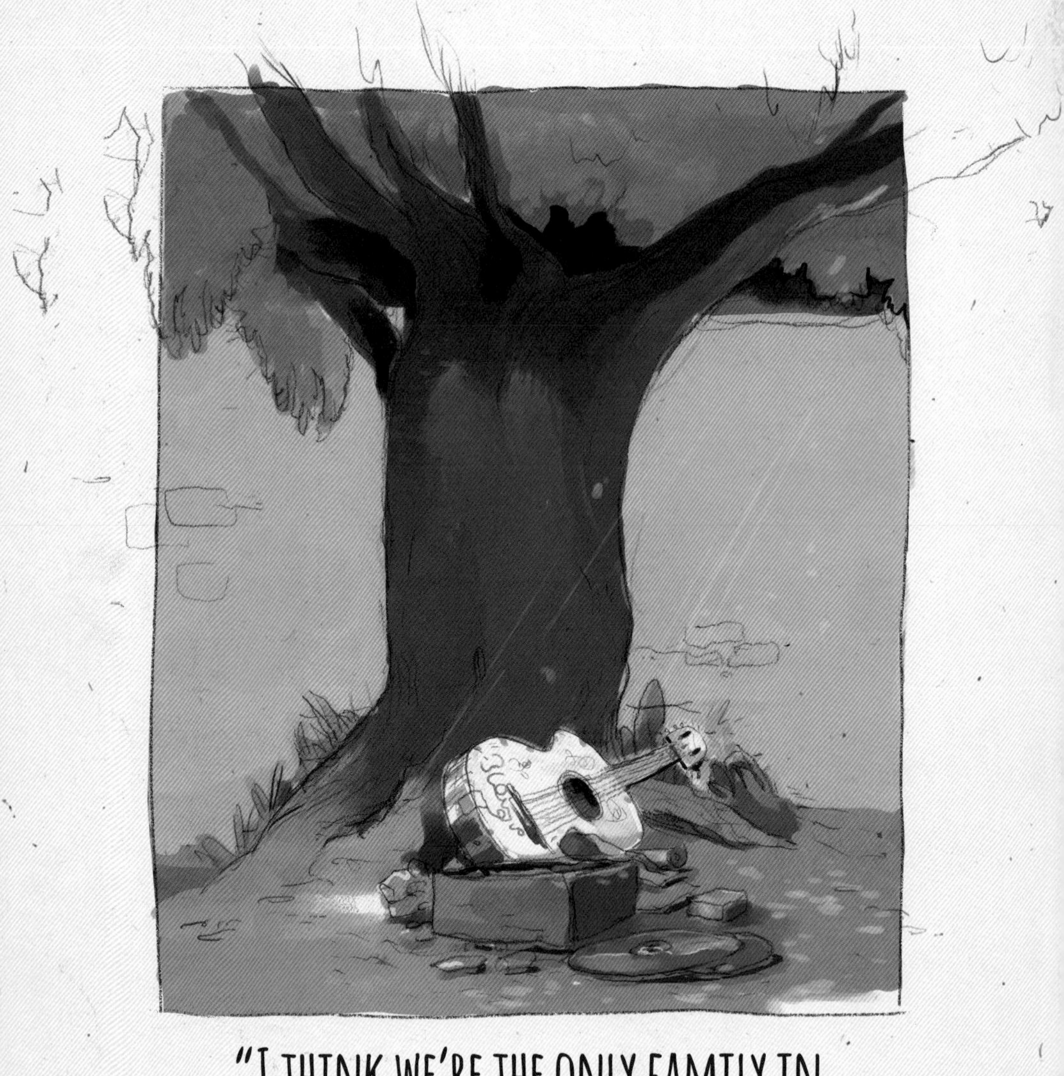

"I THINK WE'RE THE ONLY FAMILY IN MEXICO WHO HATES MUSIC."

-MIGUEL

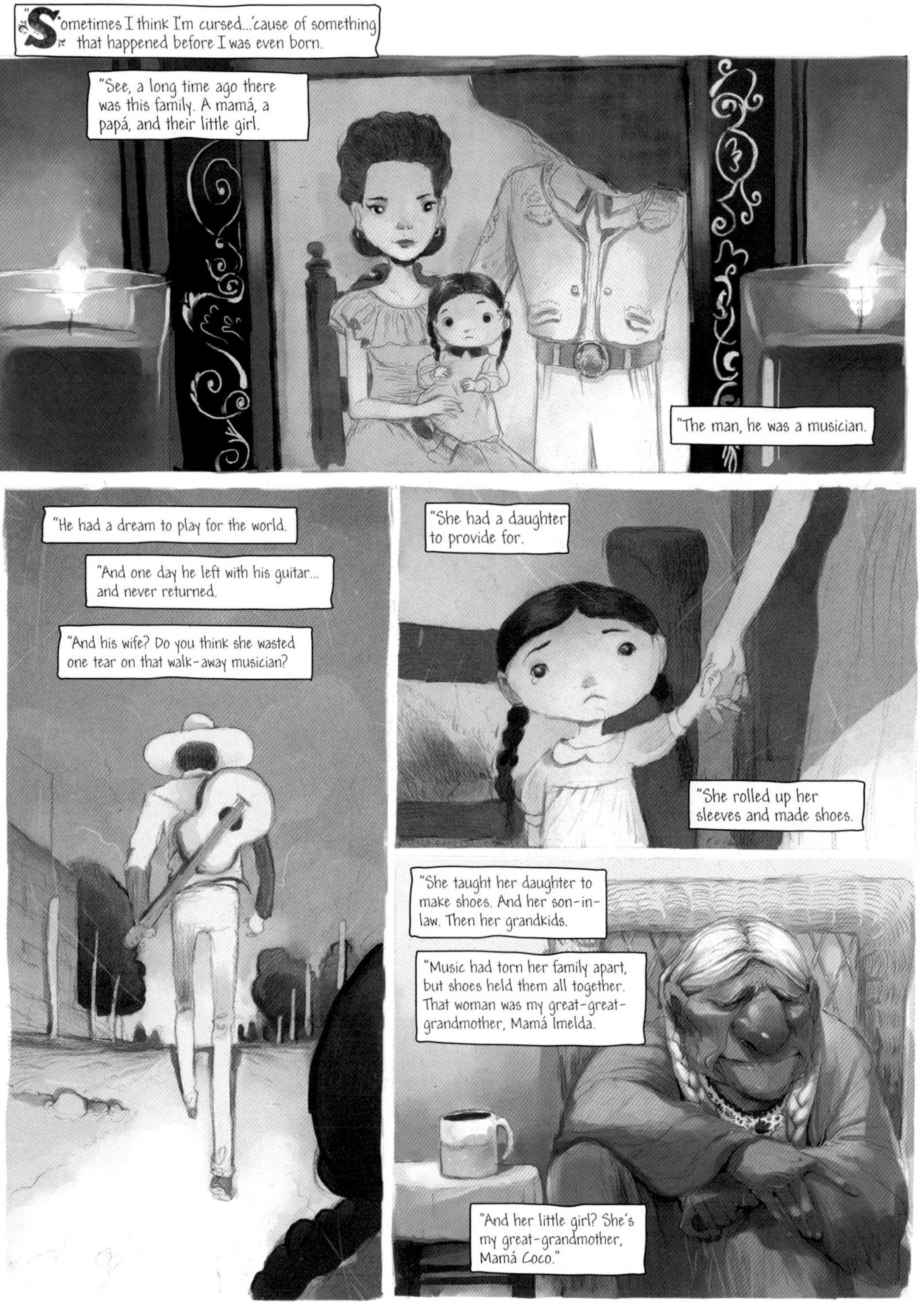
"Sometimes I think I'm cursed...'cause of something that happened before I was even born.
"See, a long time ago there was this family. A mamá, a papá, and their little girl.
"The man, he was a musician.
"He had a dream to play for the world.
"And one day he left with his guitar... and never returned.
"And his wife? Do you think she wasted one tear on that walk-away musician?
"She had a daughter to provide for.
"She rolled up her sleeves and made shoes.
"She taught her daughter to make shoes. And her son-in-law. Then her grandkids.
"Music had torn her family apart, but shoes held them all together. That woman was my great-great-grandmother, Mamá Imelda.
"And her little girl? She's my great-grandmother, Mamá Coco."

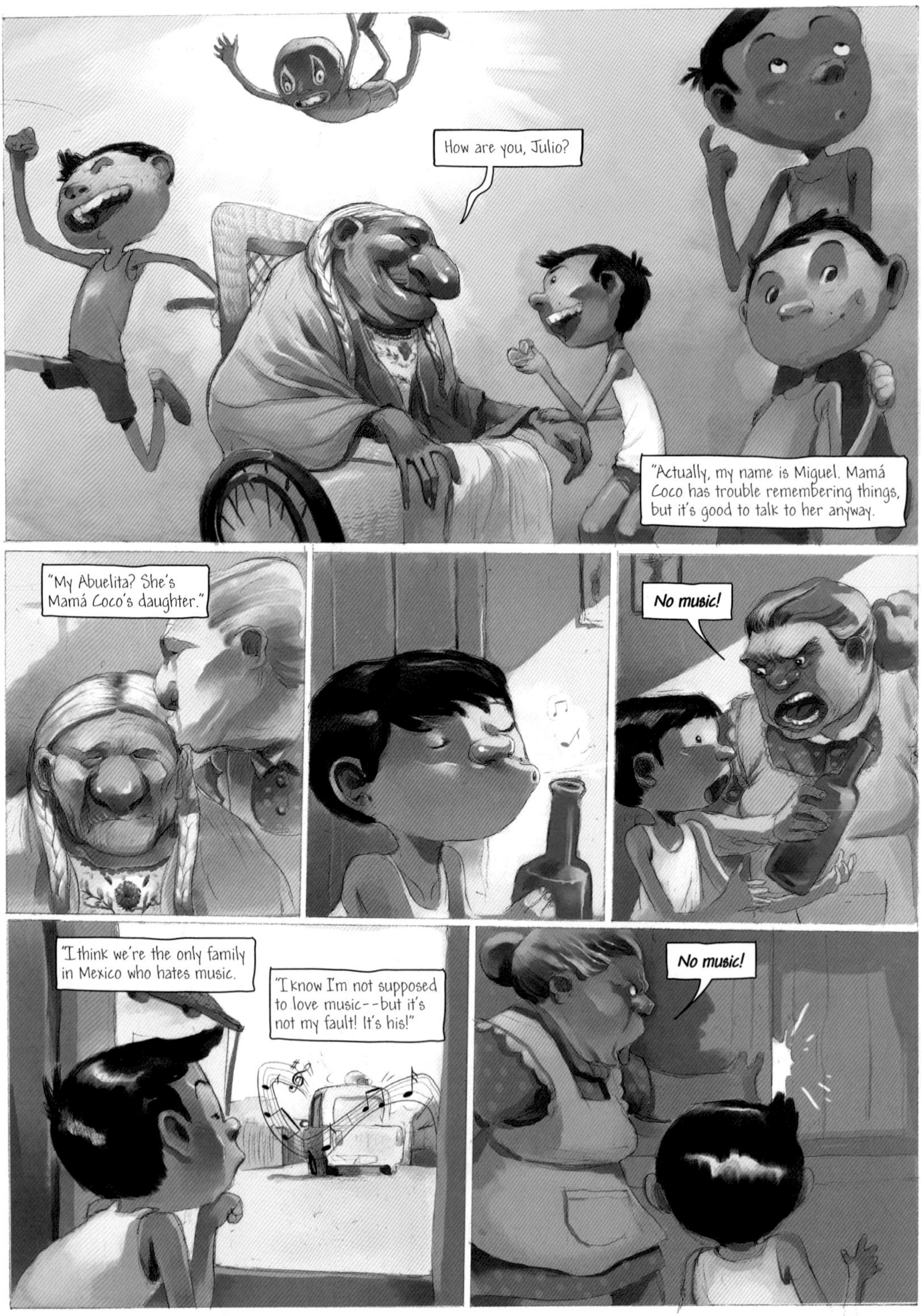

How are you, Julio?
"Actually, my name is Miguel. Mamá Coco has trouble remembering things, but it's good to talk to her anyway.
"My Abuelita? She's Mamá Coco's daughter."
No music!
"I think we're the only family in Mexico who hates music.
"I know I'm not supposed to love music--but it's not my fault! It's his!"
No music!

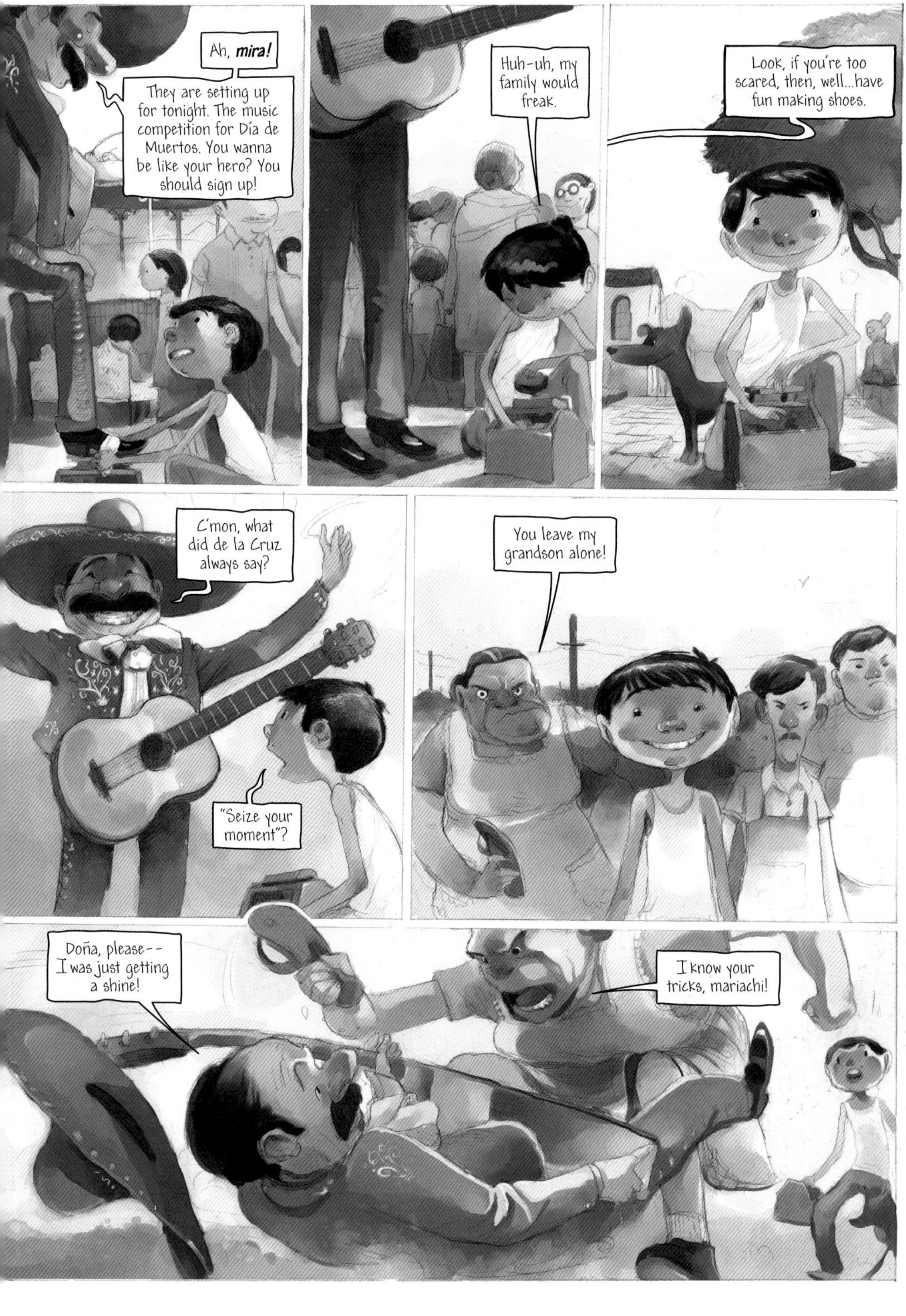
Ah, mira!
They are setting up for tonight. The music competition for Día de Muertos. You wanna be like your hero? You should sign up!
Huh-uh, my family would freak.
Look, if you're too scared, then, well...have fun making shoes.
C'mon, what did de la Cruz always say?
"Seize your moment"?
You leave my grandson alone!
Doña, please-- I was just getting a shine!
I know your tricks, mariachi!

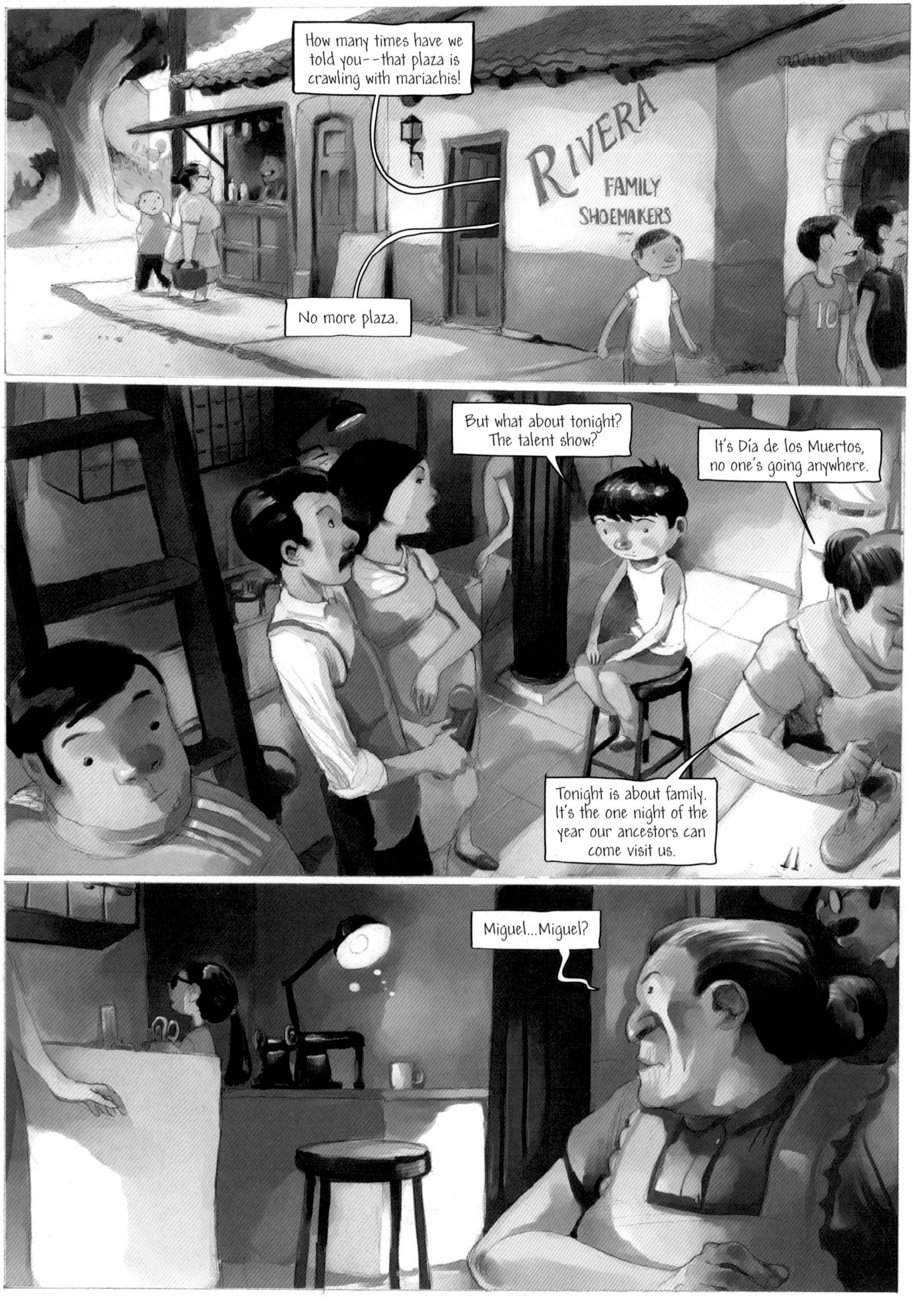
How many times have we told you--that plaza is crawling with mariachis!
No more plaza.
RIVERA FAMILY SHOEMAKERS
But what about tonight? The talent show?
It's Día de los Muertos, no one's going anywhere.
Tonight is about family. It's the one night of the year our ancestors can come visit us.
Miguel...Miguel?

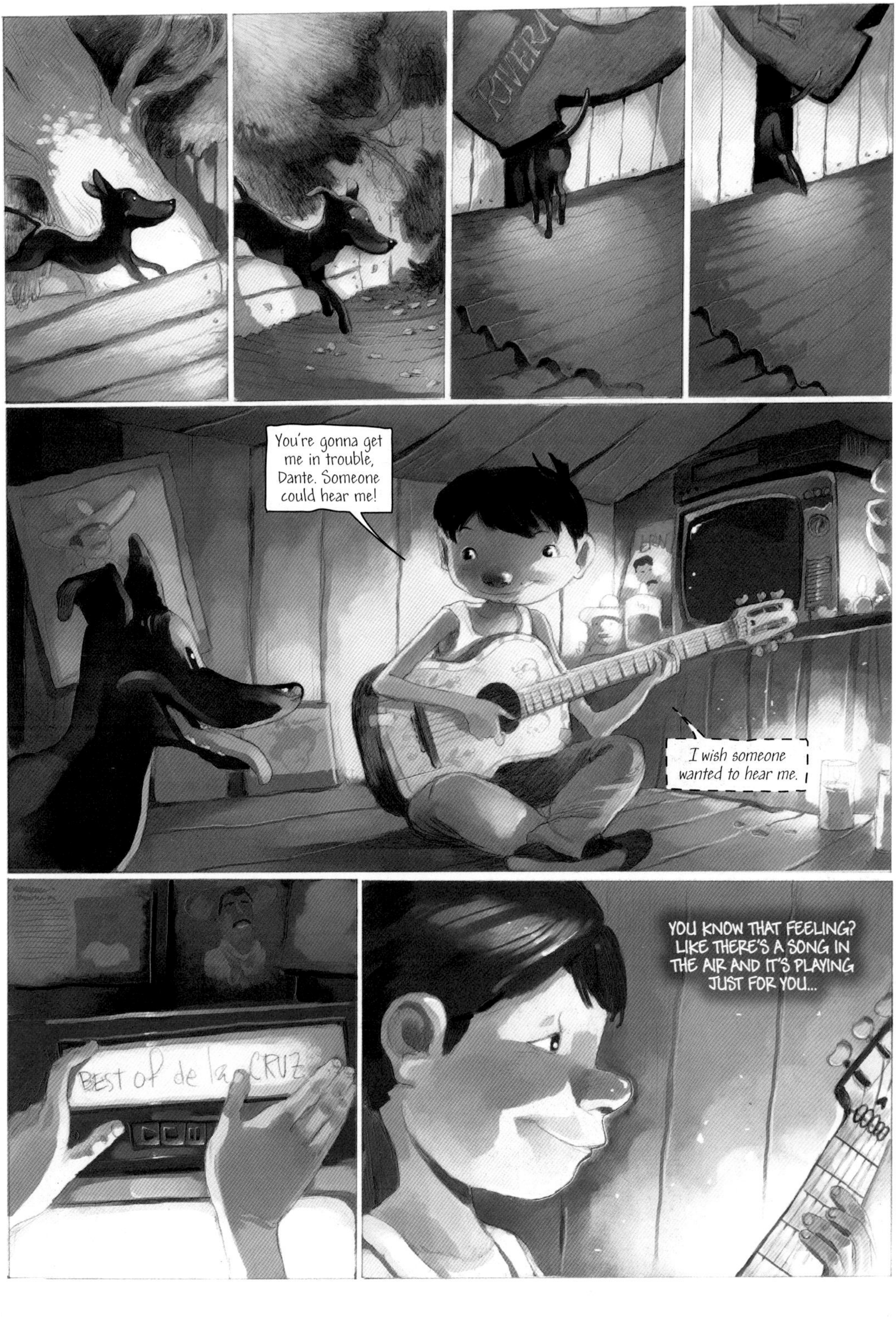
RIVERA
You're gonna get me in trouble, Dante. Someone could hear me!
I wish someone wanted to hear me.
BEST of de la CRUZ
YOU KNOW THAT FEELING? LIKE THERE'S A SONG IN THE AIR AND IT'S PLAYING JUST FOR YOU...

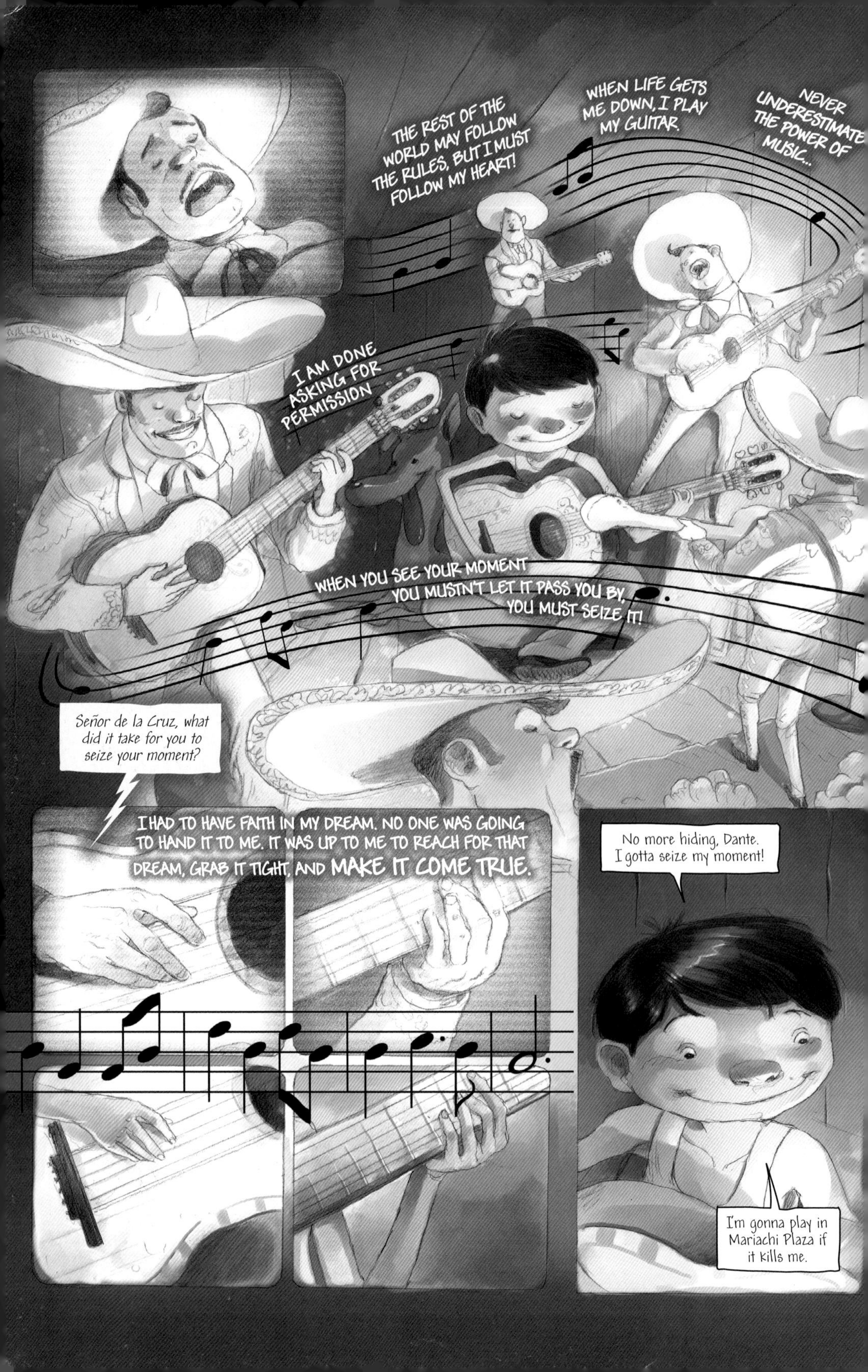
THE REST OF THE WORLD MAY FOLLOW THE RULES, BUT I MUST FOLLOW MY HEART!
WHEN LIFE GETS ME DOWN, I PLAY MY GUITAR.
NEVER UNDERESTIMATE THE POWER OF MUSIC...
I AM DONE ASKING FOR PERMISSION
WHEN YOU SEE YOUR MOMENT YOU MUSTN'T LET IT PASS YOU BY, YOU MUST SEIZE IT!
Señor de la Cruz, what did it take for you to seize your moment?
I HAD TO HAVE FAITH IN MY DREAM. NO ONE WAS GOING TO HAND IT TO ME. IT WAS UP TO ME TO REACH FOR THAT DREAM, GRAB IT TIGHT, AND MAKE IT COME TRUE.
No more hiding, Dante. I gotta seize my moment!
I'm gonna play in Mariachi Plaza if it kills me.

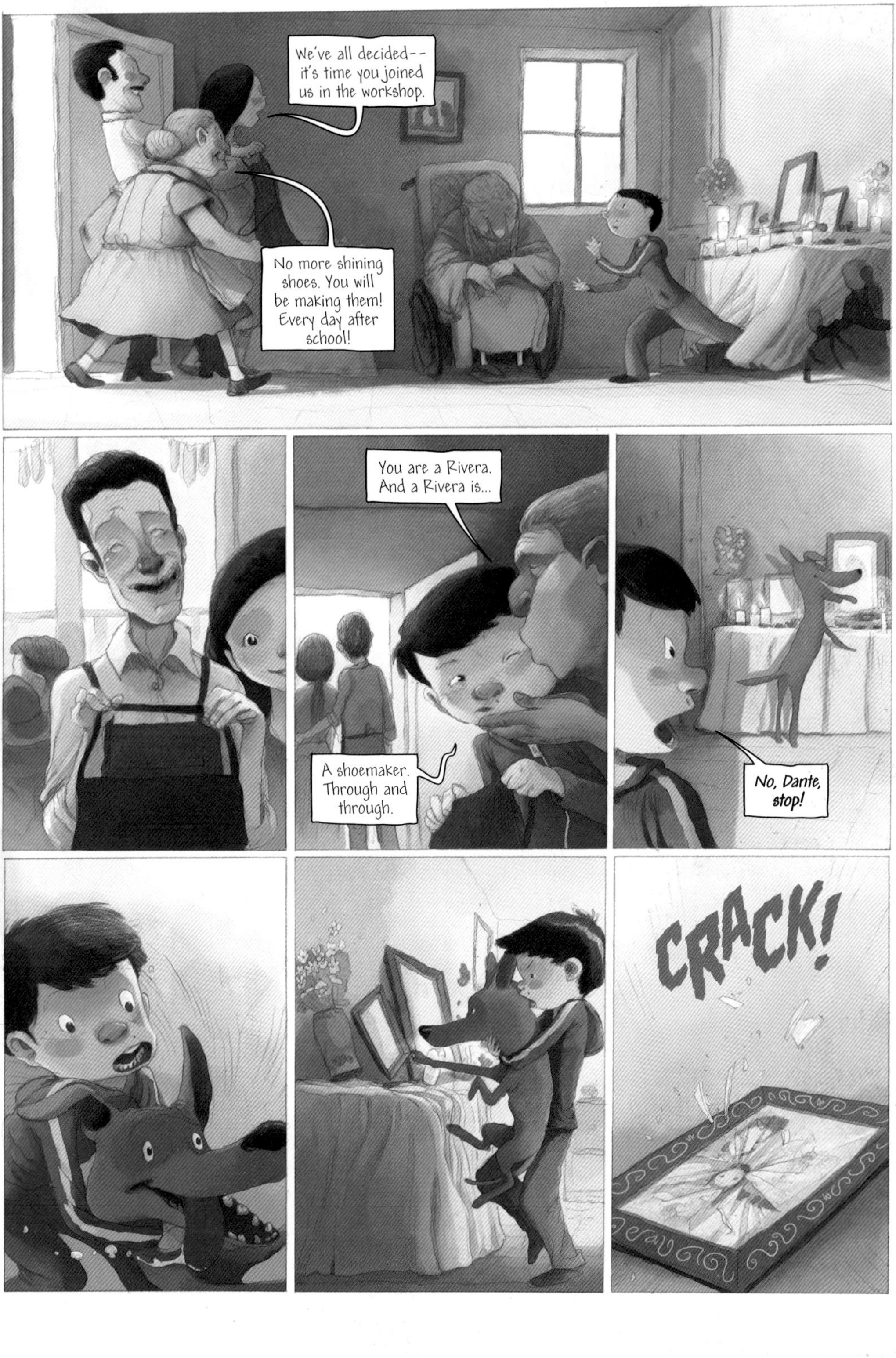
We've all decided-- it's time you joined us in the workshop.
No more shining shoes. You will be making them! Every day after school!
You are a Rivera. And a Rivera is...
A shoemaker. Through and through.
No, Dante, stop!
CRACK!

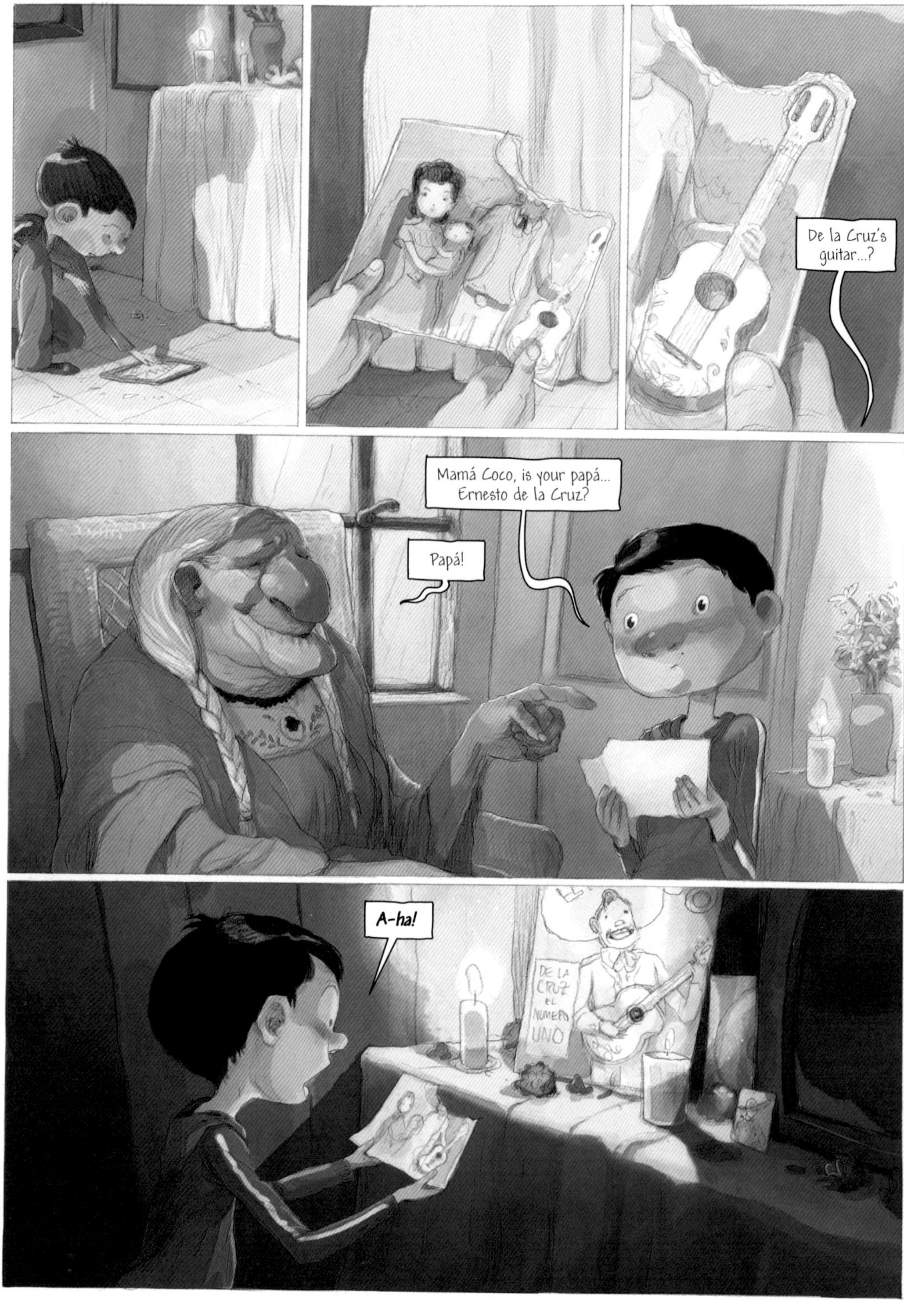
De la Cruz's guitar...?
Mamá Coco, is your papá... Ernesto de la Cruz?
Papá!
A-ha!
DE LA CRUZ EL NUMERO UNO

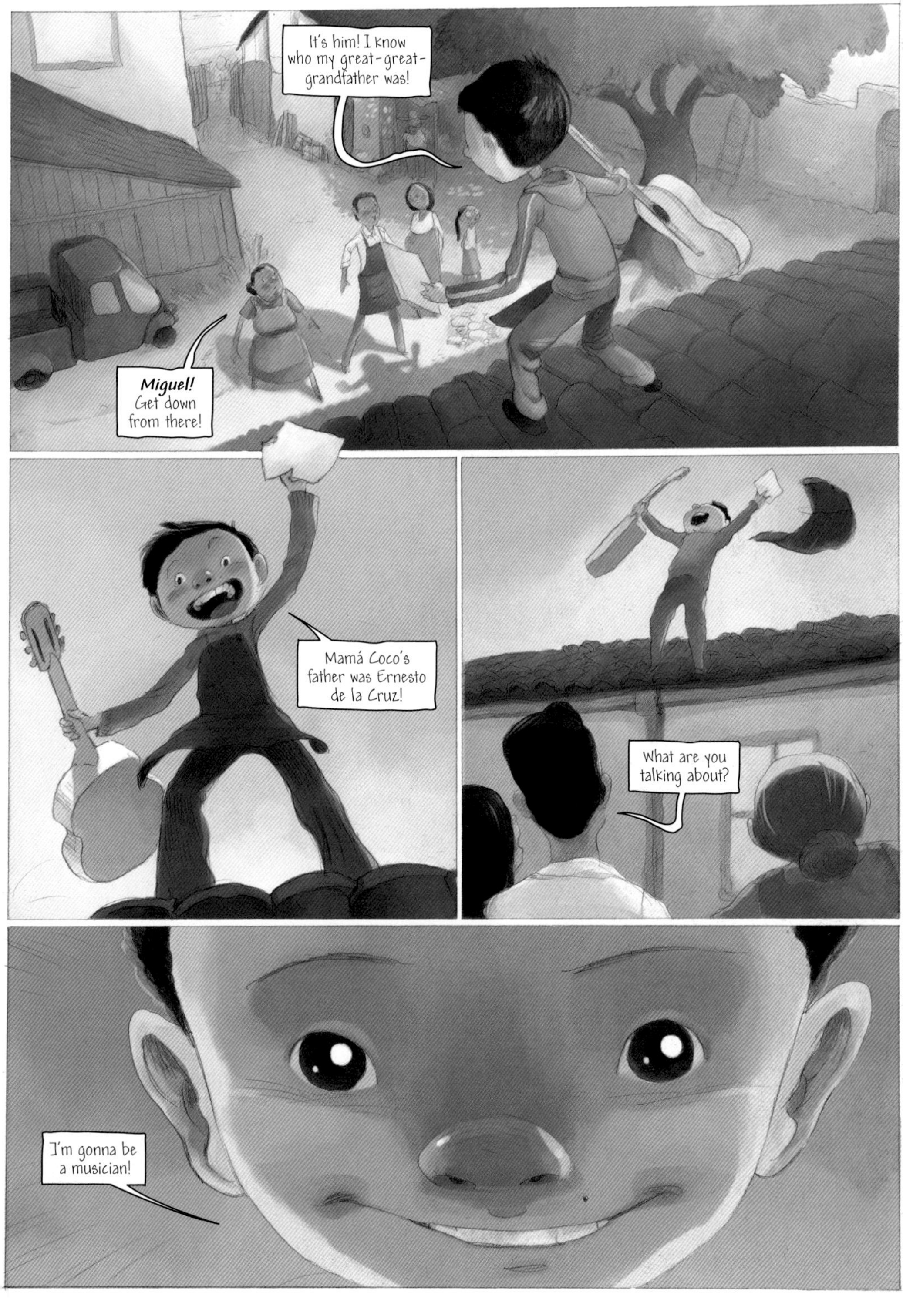
It's him! I know who my great-great-grandfather was!
Miguel! Get down from there!
Mamá Coco's father was Ernesto de la Cruz!
What are you talking about?
I'm gonna be a musician!

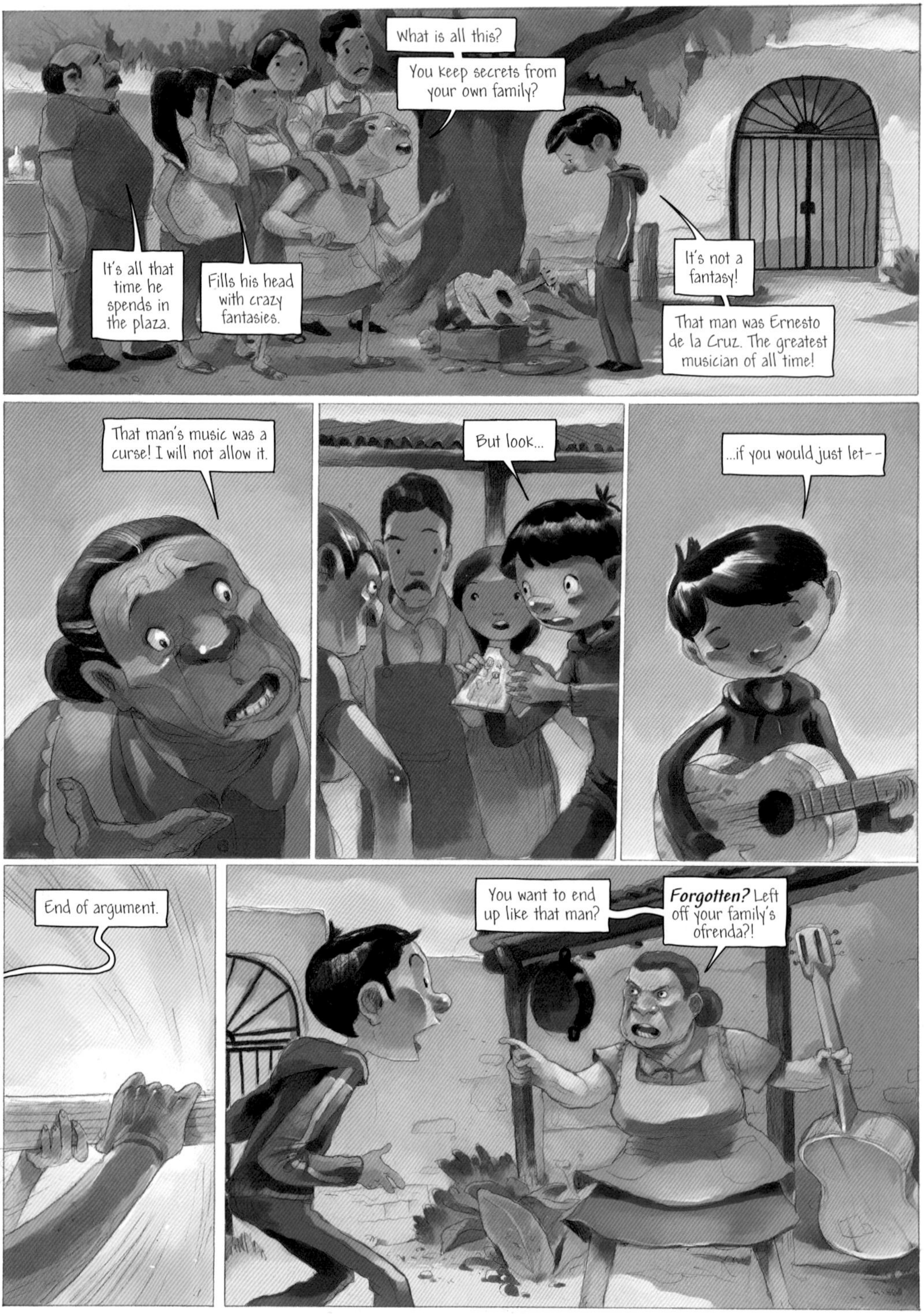
What is all this?
You keep secrets from your own family?
It's all that time he spends in the plaza.
Fills his head with crazy fantasies.
It's not a fantasy!
That man was Ernesto de la Cruz. The greatest musician of all time!
That man's music was a curse! I will not allow it.
But look...
...if you would just let--
End of argument.
You want to end up like that man?
Forgotten? Left off your family's ofrenda?!

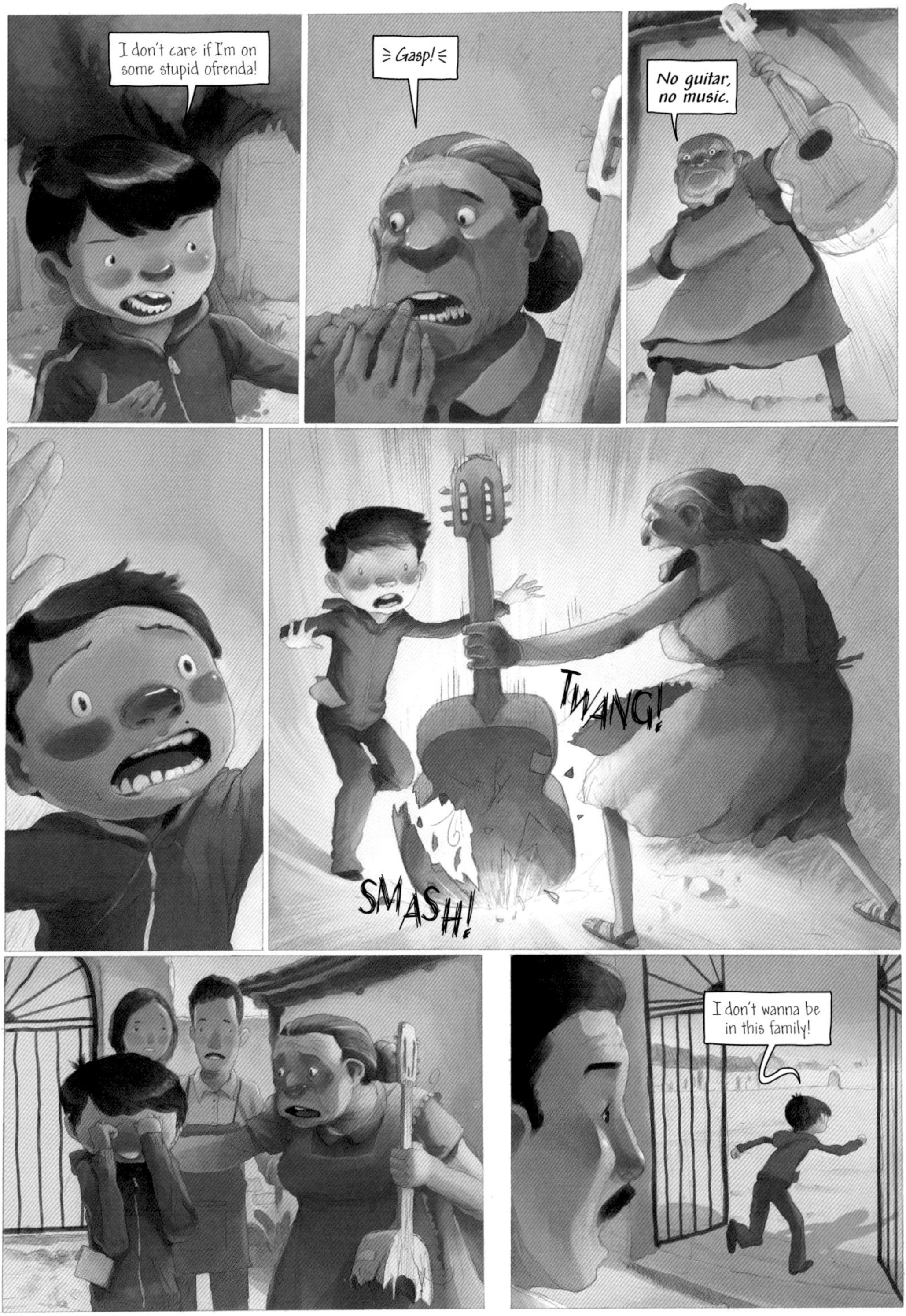
I don't care if I'm on some stupid ofrenda!
Gasp!
No guitar, no music.
TWANG!
SMASH!
I don't wanna be in this family!

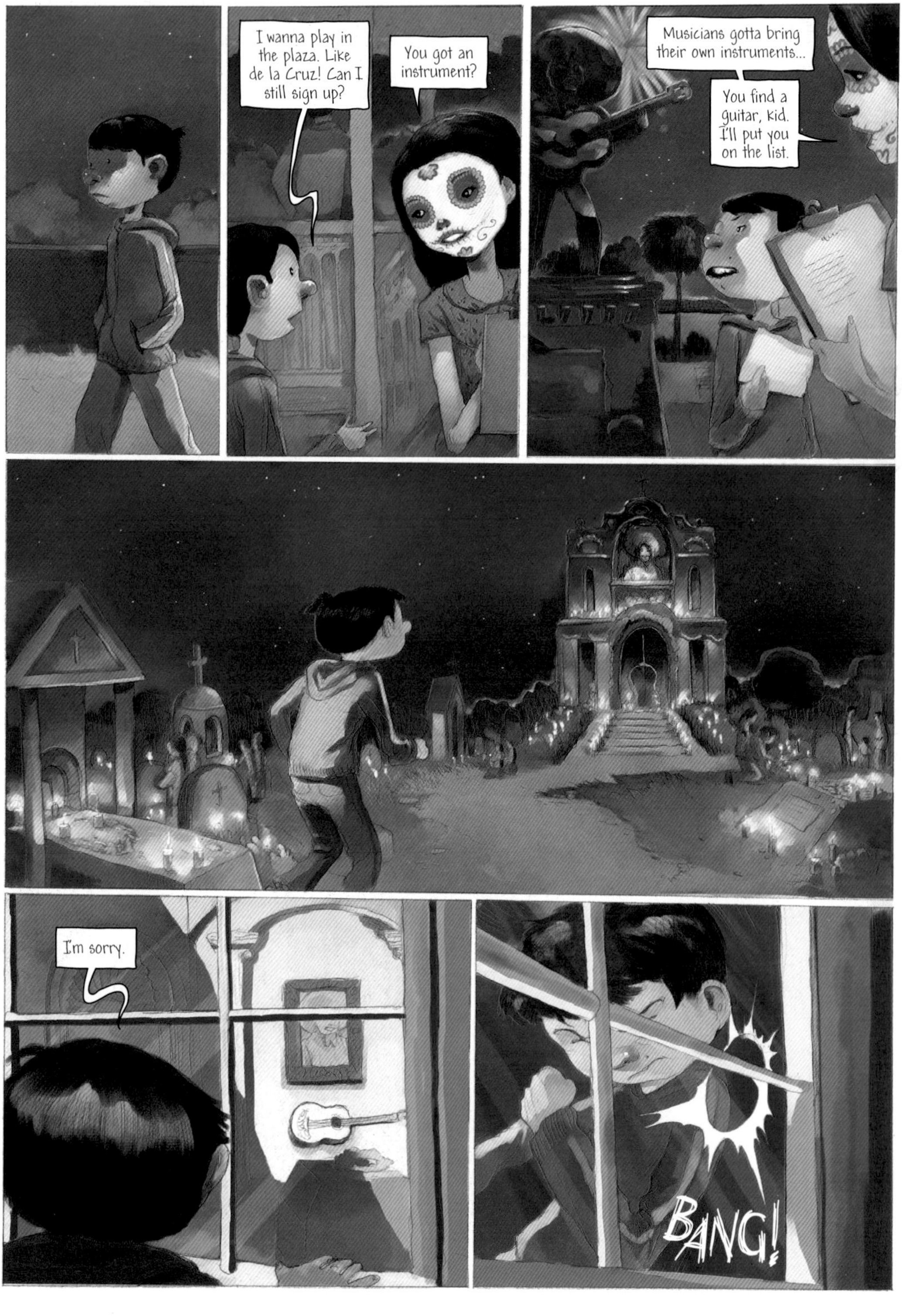
I wanna play in the plaza. Like de la Cruz! Can I still sign up?
You got an instrument?
Musicians gotta bring their own instruments...
You find a guitar, kid. I'll put you on the list.
I'm sorry.
BANG!

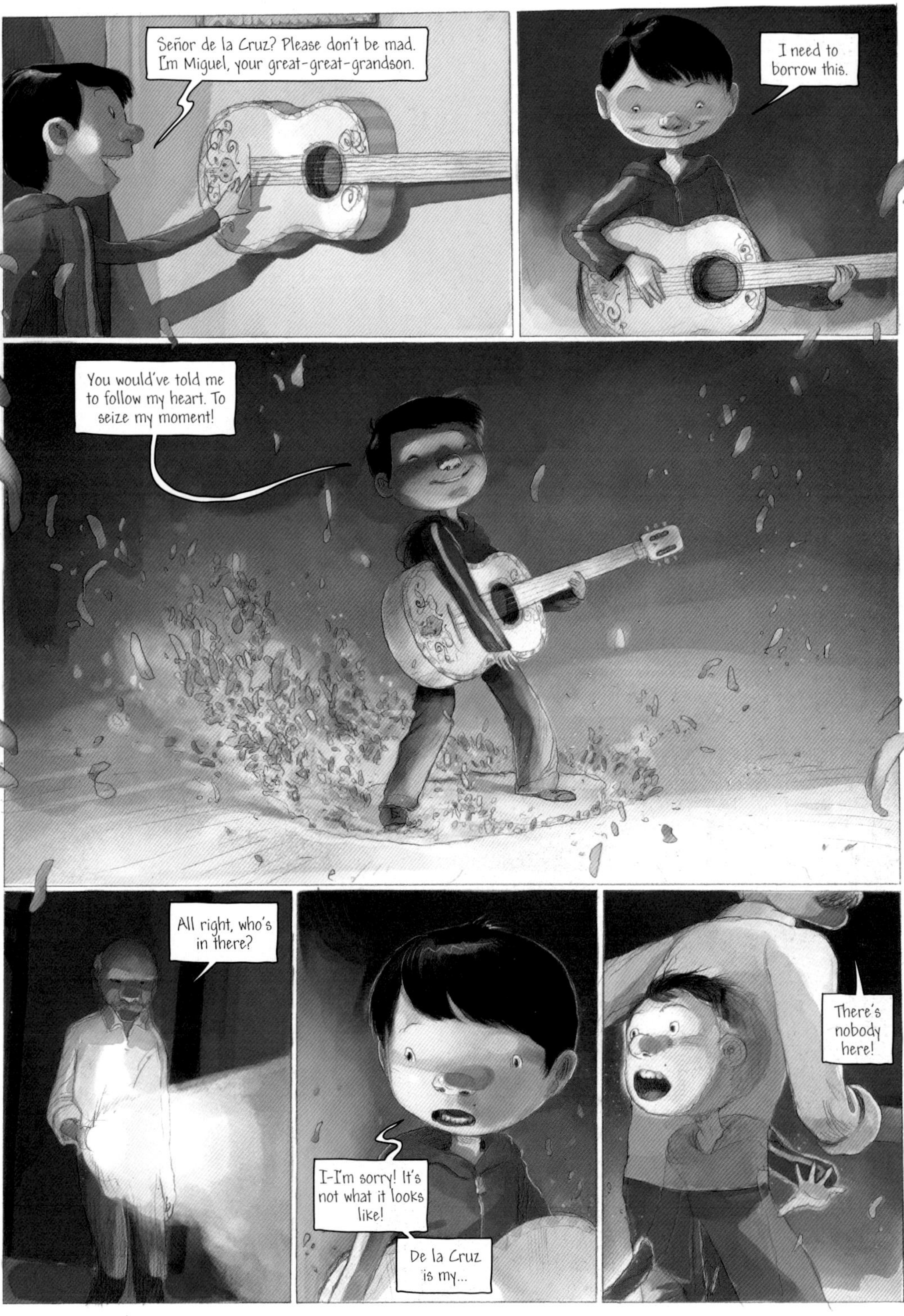
Señor de la Cruz? Please don't be mad. I'm Miguel, your great-great-grandson.
I need to borrow this.
You would've told me to follow my heart. To seize my moment!
All right, who's in there?
I-I'm sorry! It's not what it looks like!
De la Cruz is my...
There's nobody here!

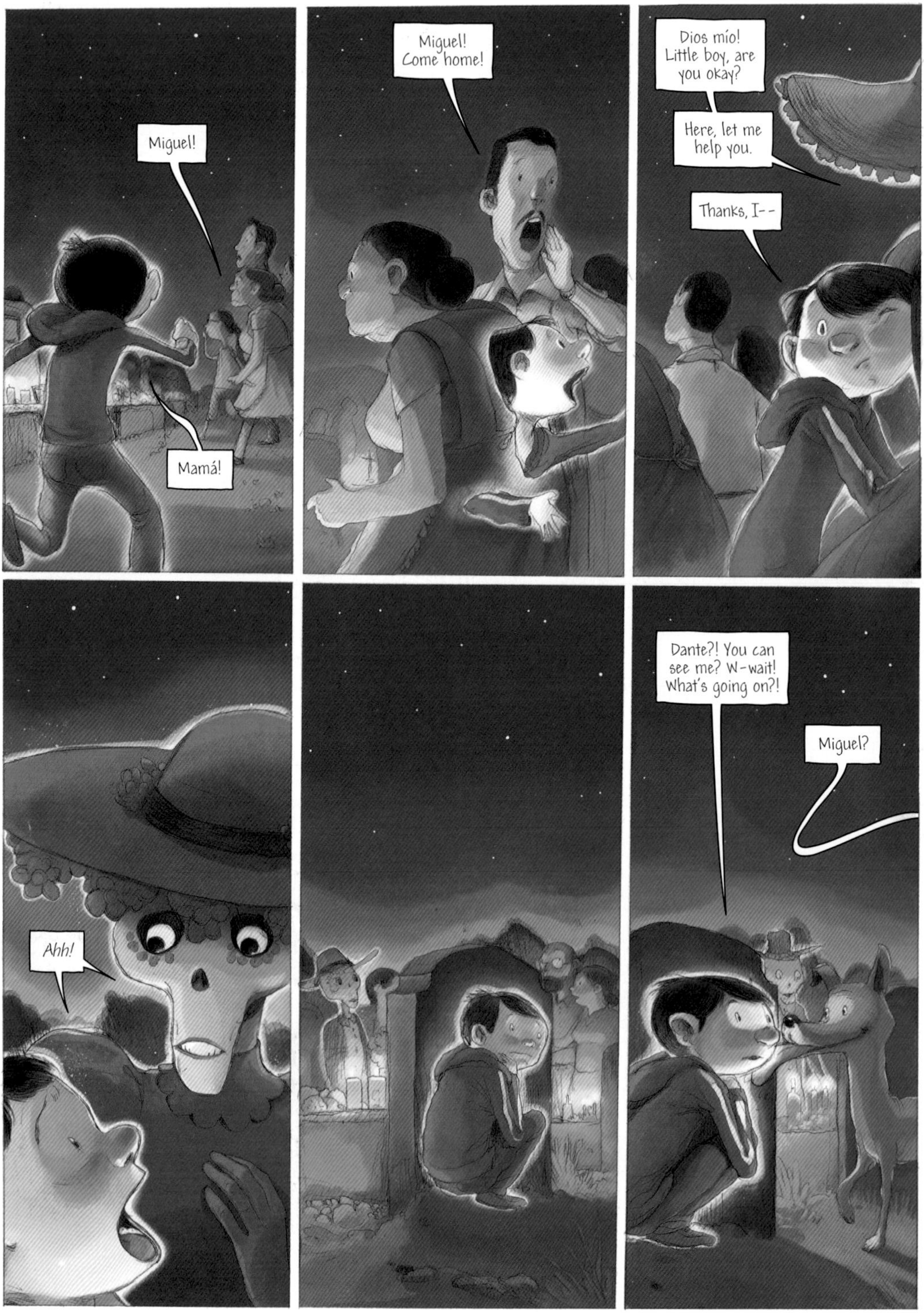

Miguel!
Mamá!
Miguel! Come home!
Dios mío! Little boy, are you okay?
Here, let me help you.
Thanks, I--
Ahh!
Dante?! You can see me? W-wait! What's going on?!
Miguel?

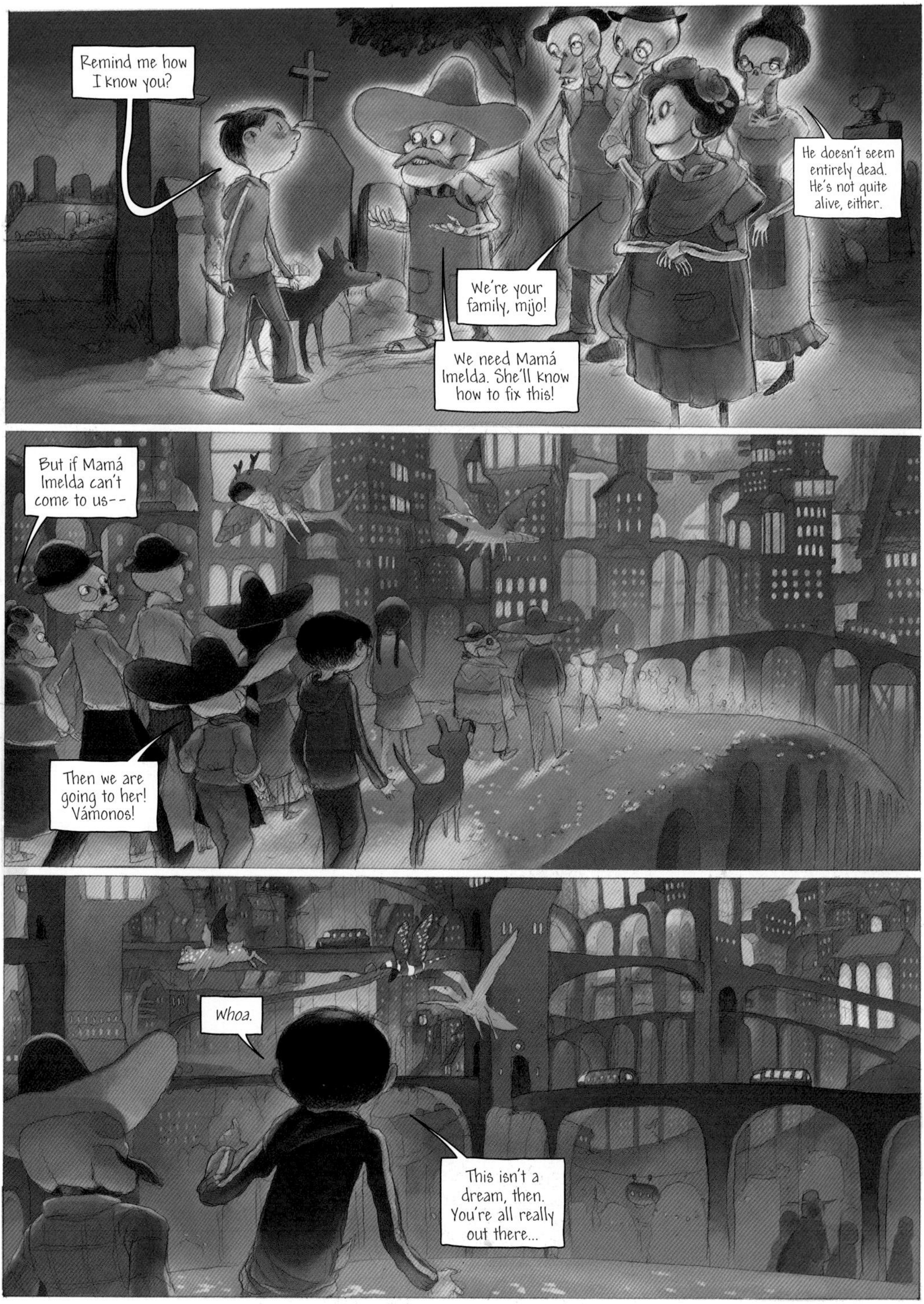
Remind me how I know you?
He doesn't seem entirely dead. He's not quite alive, either.
We're your family, mijo!
We need Mamá Imelda. She'll know how to fix this!
But if Mamá Imelda can't come to us--
Then we are going to her! Vámonos!
Whoa.
This isn't a dream, then. You're all really out there...

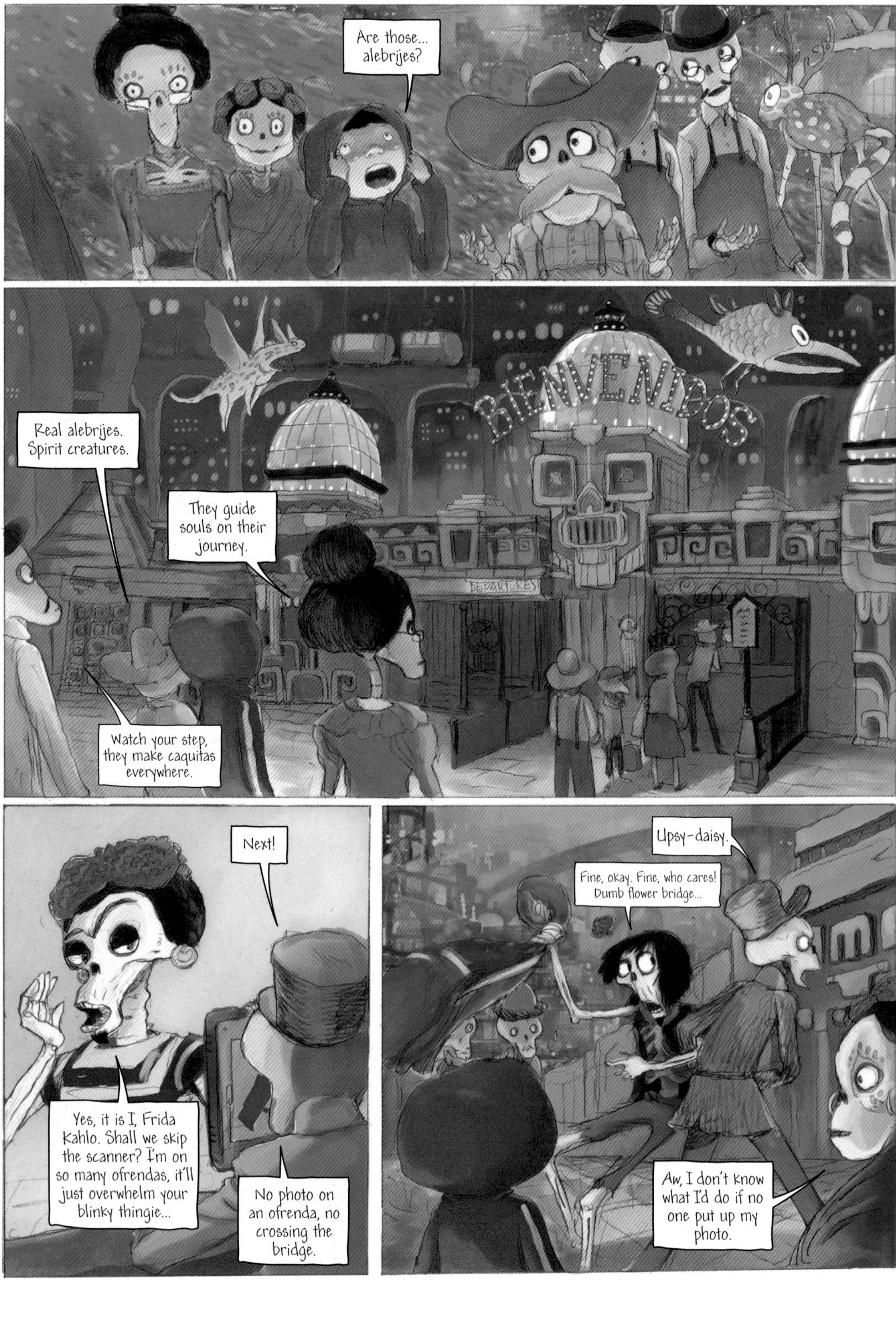
Are those... alebrijes?
Real alebrijes. Spirit creatures.
They guide souls on their journey.
Watch your step, they make caquitas everywhere.
BIENVENIDOS
DEPARTURES
Next!
Yes, it is I, Frida Kahlo. Shall we skip the scanner? I'm on so many ofrendas, it'll just overwhelm your blinky thingie...
No photo on an ofrenda, no crossing the bridge.
Upsy-daisy.
Fine, okay. Fine, who cares! Dumb flower bridge...
Aw, I don't know what I'd do if no one put up my photo.

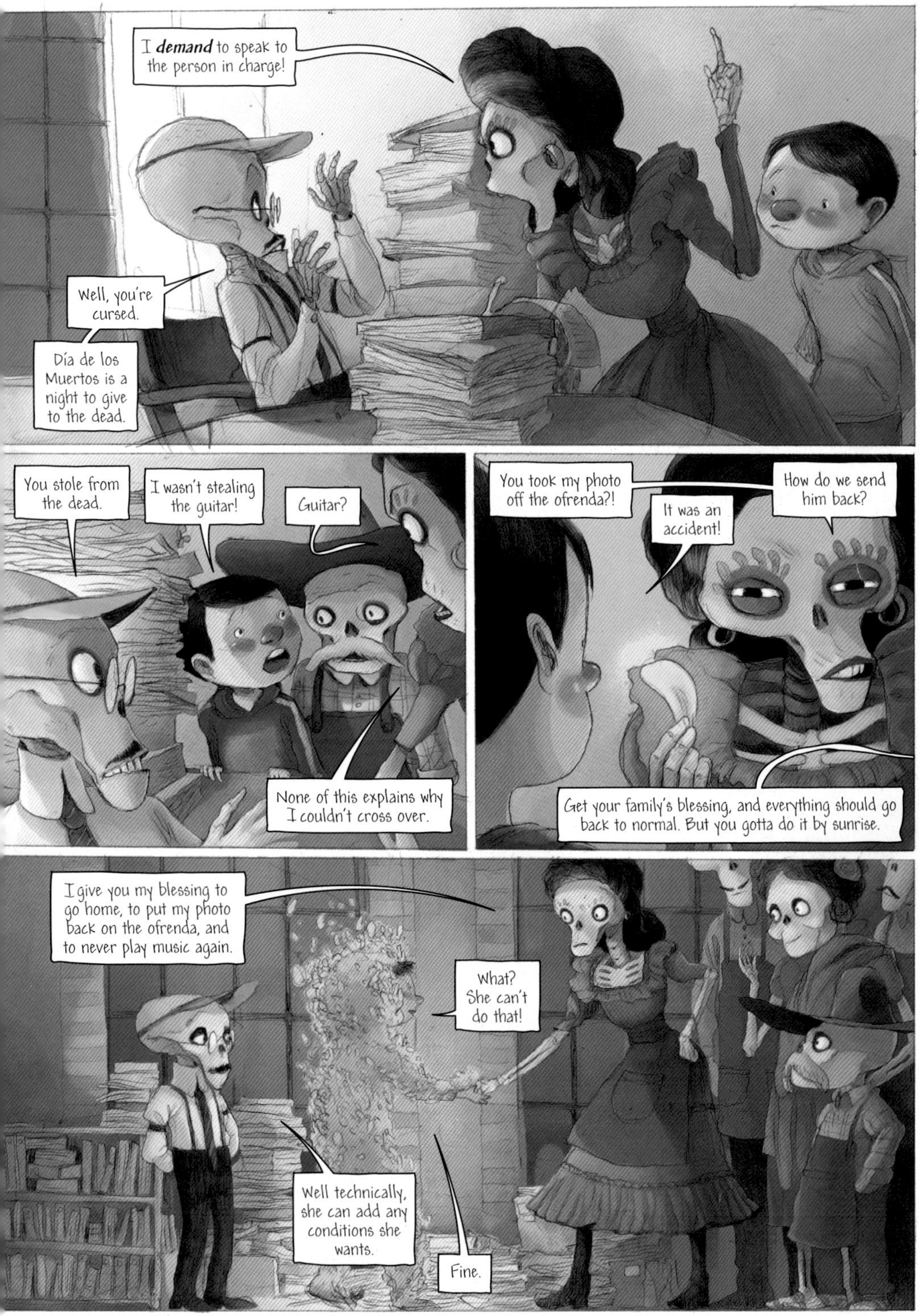
I **demand** to speak to the person in charge!
Well, you're cursed.
Día de los Muertos is a night to give to the dead.
You stole from the dead.
I wasn't stealing the guitar!
Guitar?
None of this explains why I couldn't cross over.
You took my photo off the ofrenda?!
It was an accident!
How do we send him back?
Get your family's blessing, and everything should go back to normal. But you gotta do it by sunrise.
I give you my blessing to go home, to put my photo back on the ofrenda, and to never play music again.
What? She can't do that!
Well technically, she can add any conditions she wants.
Fine.

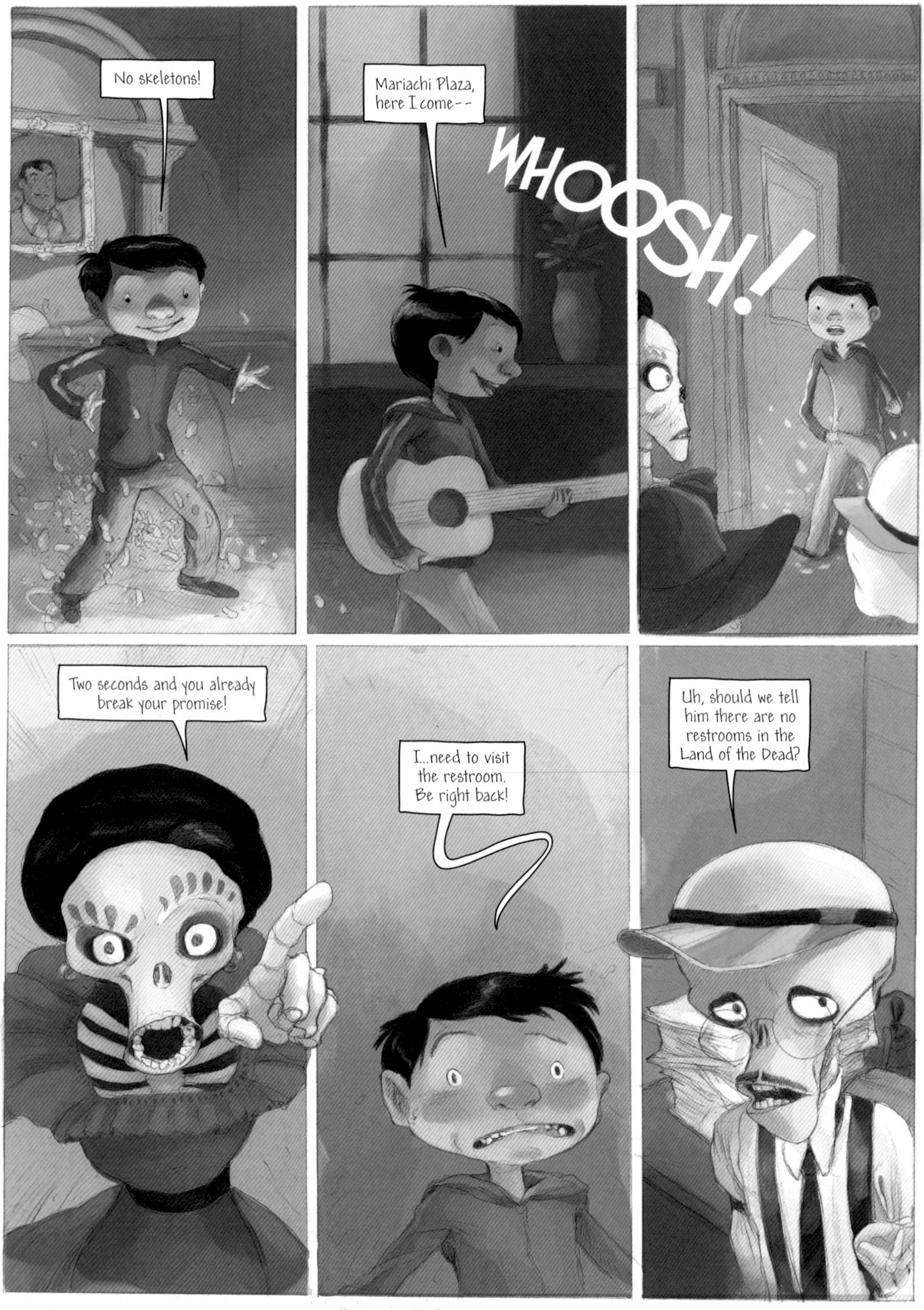
No skeletons!
Mariachi Plaza, here I come--
WHOOSH!
Two seconds and you already break your promise!
I...need to visit the restroom. Be right back!
Uh, should we tell him there are no restrooms in the Land of the Dead?

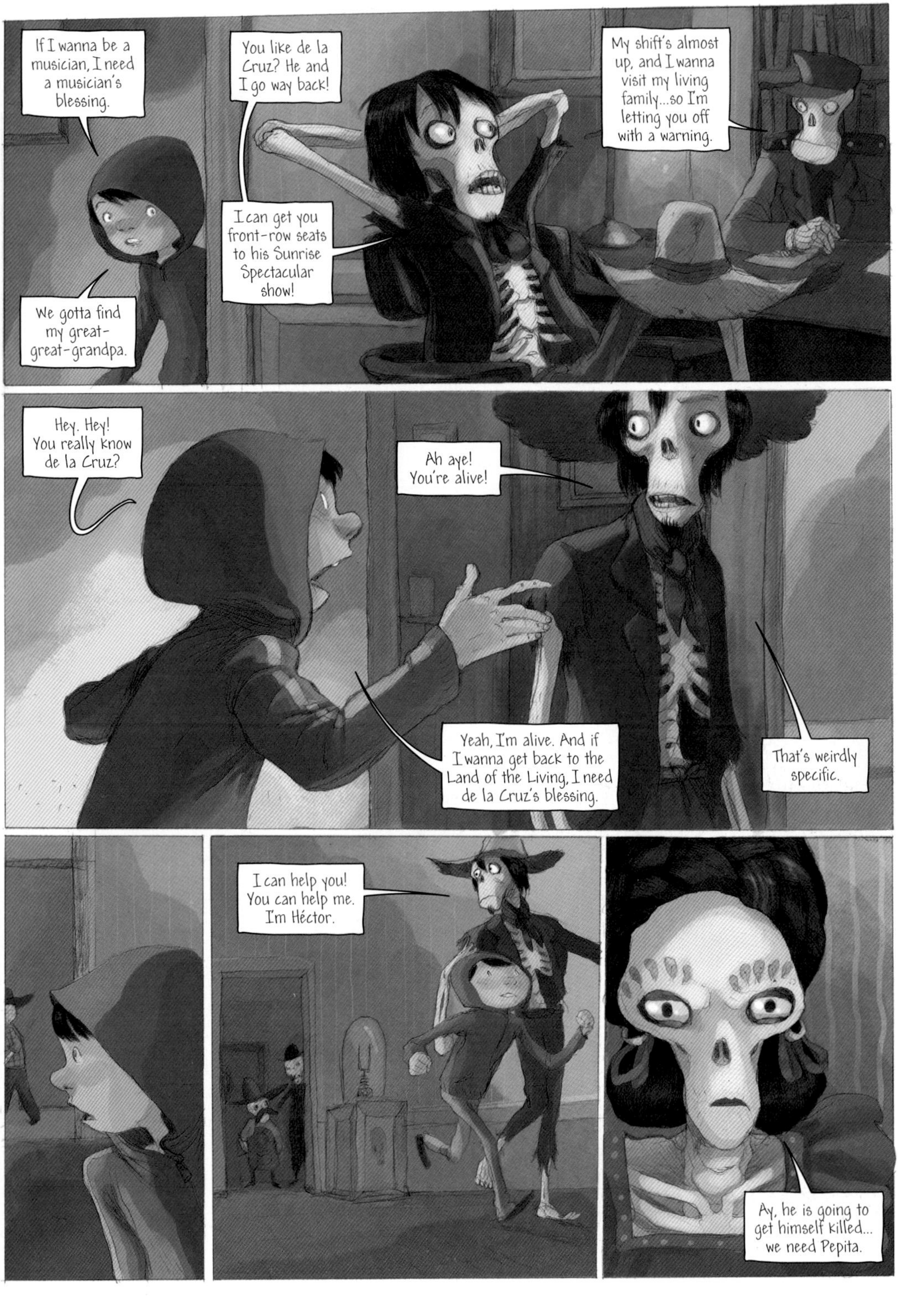
If I wanna be a musician, I need a musician's blessing.
We gotta find my great-great-grandpa.
You like de la Cruz? He and I go way back!
I can get you front-row seats to his Sunrise Spectacular show!
My shift's almost up, and I wanna visit my living family...so I'm letting you off with a warning.
Hey. Hey! You really know de la Cruz?
Ah aye! You're alive!
Yeah, I'm alive. And if I wanna get back to the Land of the Living, I need de la Cruz's blessing.
That's weirdly specific.
I can help you! You can help me. I'm Héctor.
Ay, he is going to get himself killed... we need Pepita.

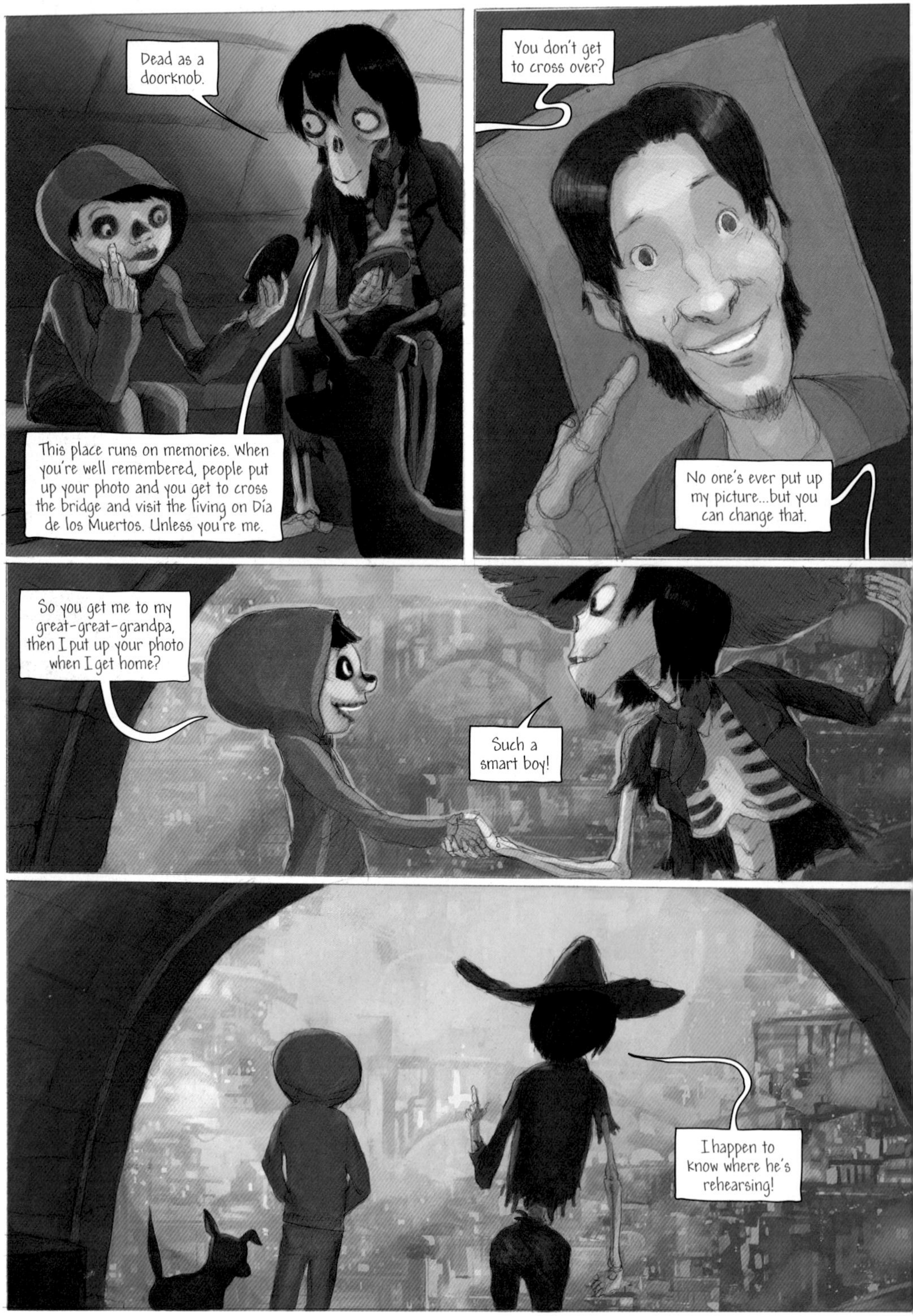
Dead as a doorknob.
This place runs on memories. When you're well remembered, people put up your photo and you get to cross the bridge and visit the living on Día de los Muertos. Unless you're me.
You don't get to cross over?
No one's ever put up my picture...but you can change that.
So you get me to my great-great-grandpa, then I put up your photo when I get home?
Such a smart boy!
I happen to know where he's rehearsing!

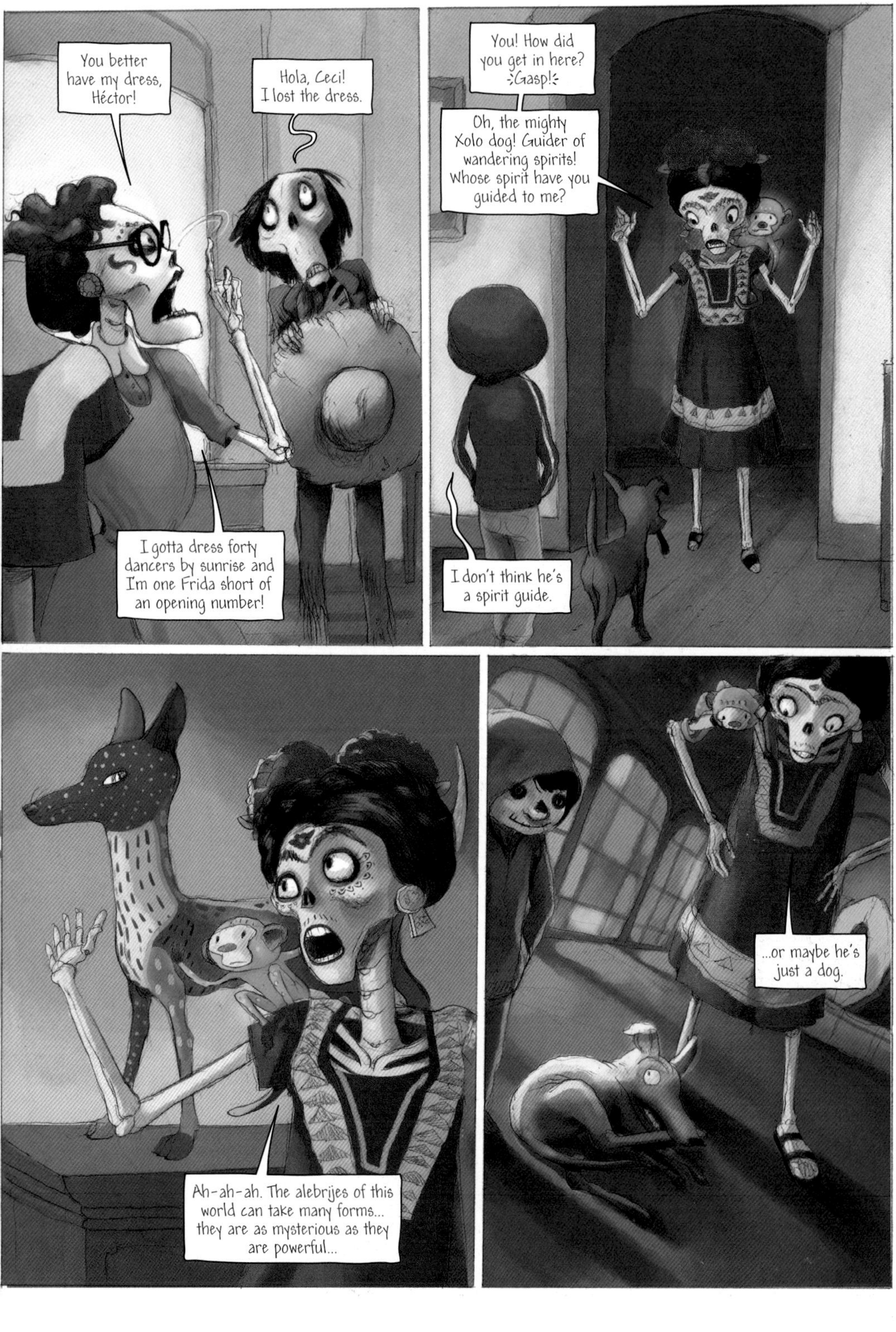
You better have my dress, Héctor!
Hola, Ceci! I lost the dress.
I gotta dress forty dancers by sunrise and I'm one Frida short of an opening number!
You! How did you get in here? Gasp!
Oh, the mighty Xolo dog! Guider of wandering spirits! Whose spirit have you guided to me?
I don't think he's a spirit guide.
Ah-ah-ah. The alebrijes of this world can take many forms... they are as mysterious as they are powerful...
...or maybe he's just a dog.

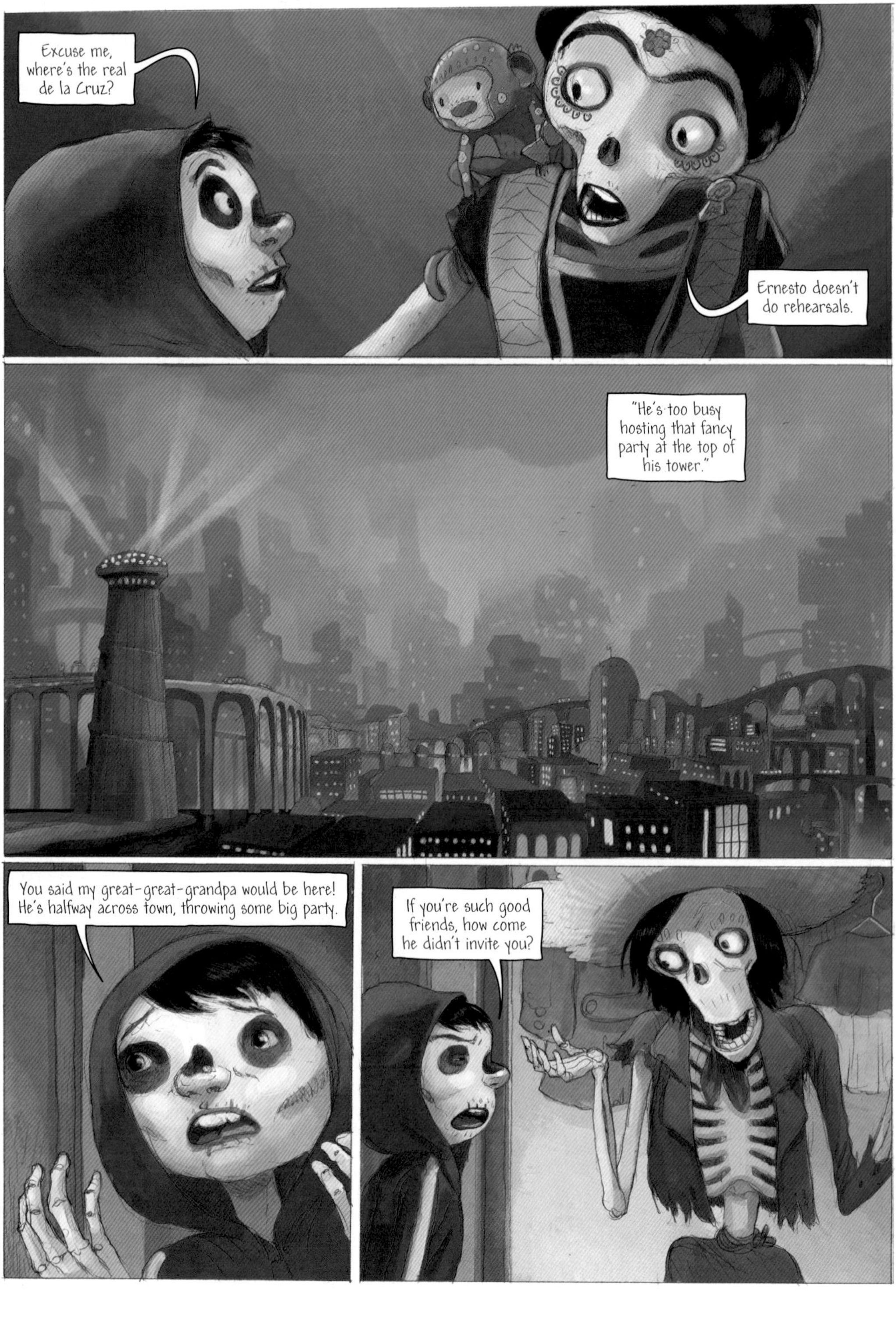
Excuse me, where's the real de la Cruz?
Ernesto doesn't do rehearsals.
"He's too busy hosting that fancy party at the top of his tower."
You said my great-great-grandpa would be here! He's halfway across town, throwing some big party.
If you're such good friends, how come he didn't invite you?

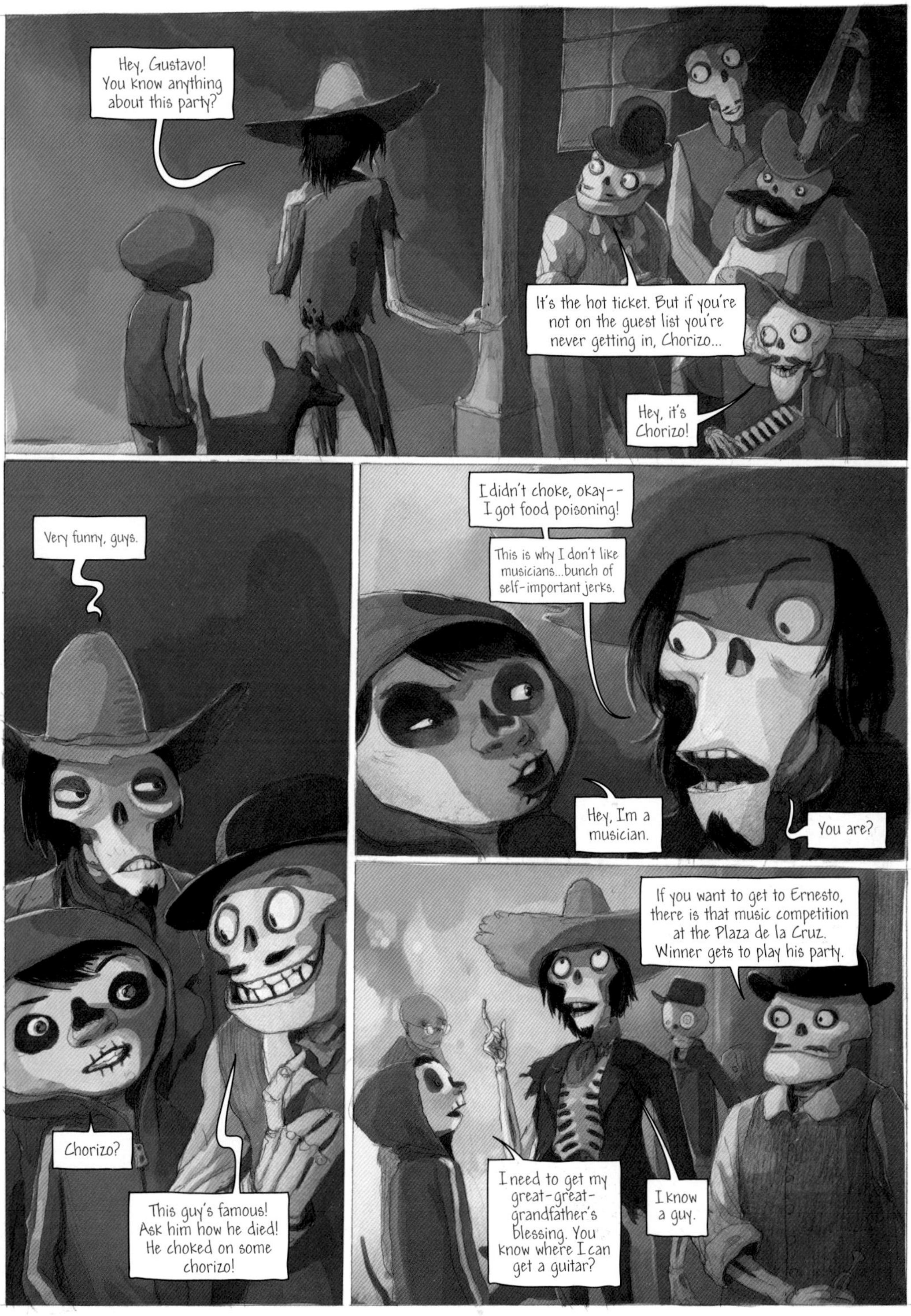
Hey, Gustavo! You know anything about this party?
It's the hot ticket. But if you're not on the guest list you're never getting in, Chorizo...
Hey, it's Chorizo!
Very funny, guys.
Chorizo?
This guy's famous! Ask him how he died! He choked on some chorizo!
I didn't choke, okay-- I got food poisoning!
This is why I don't like musicians...bunch of self-important jerks.
Hey, I'm a musician.
You are?
I need to get my great-great-grandfather's blessing. You know where I can get a guitar?
I know a guy.
If you want to get to Ernesto, there is that music competition at the Plaza de la Cruz. Winner gets to play his party.

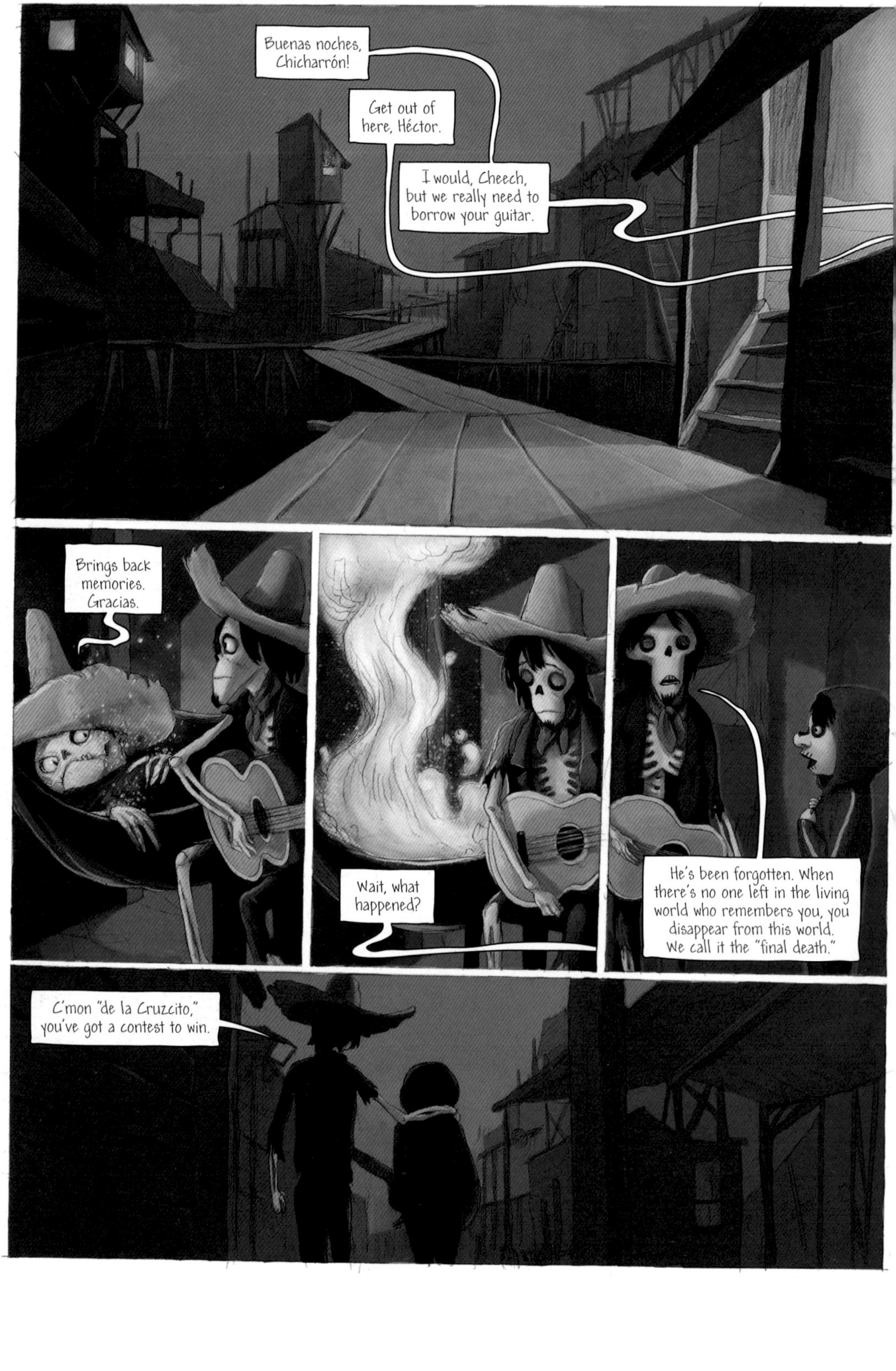

Buenas noches, Chicharrón!
Get out of here, Héctor.
I would, Cheech, but we really need to borrow your guitar.
Brings back memories. Gracias.
Wait, what happened?
He's been forgotten. When there's no one left in the living world who remembers you, you disappear from this world. We call it the "final death."
C'mon "de la Cruzcito," you've got a contest to win.

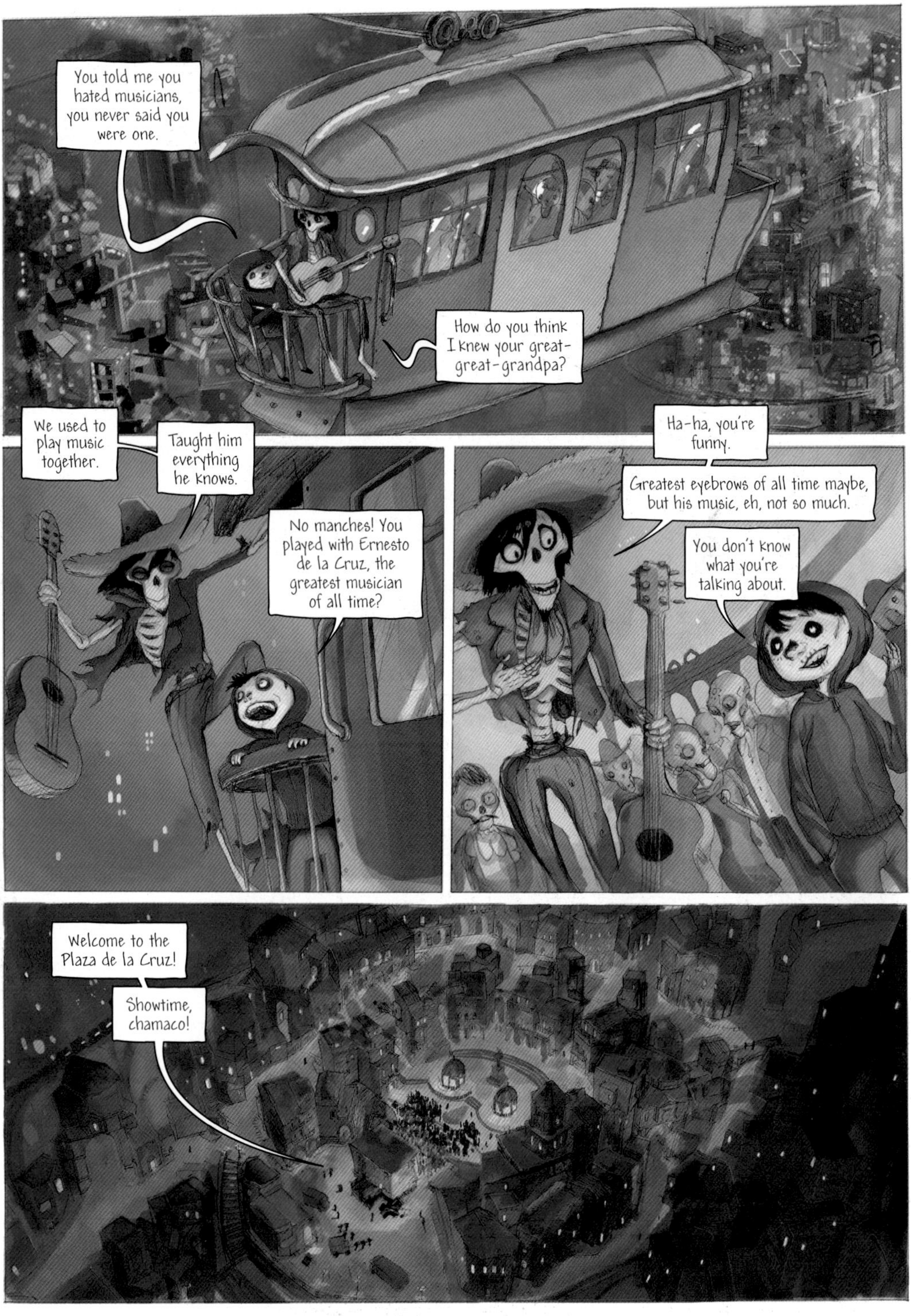
You told me you hated musicians, you never said you were one.
How do you think I knew your great-great-grandpa?
We used to play music together.
Taught him everything he knows.
No manches! You played with Ernesto de la Cruz, the greatest musician of all time?
Ha-ha, you're funny.
Greatest eyebrows of all time maybe, but his music, eh, not so much.
You don't know what you're talking about.
Welcome to the Plaza de la Cruz!
Showtime, chamaco!

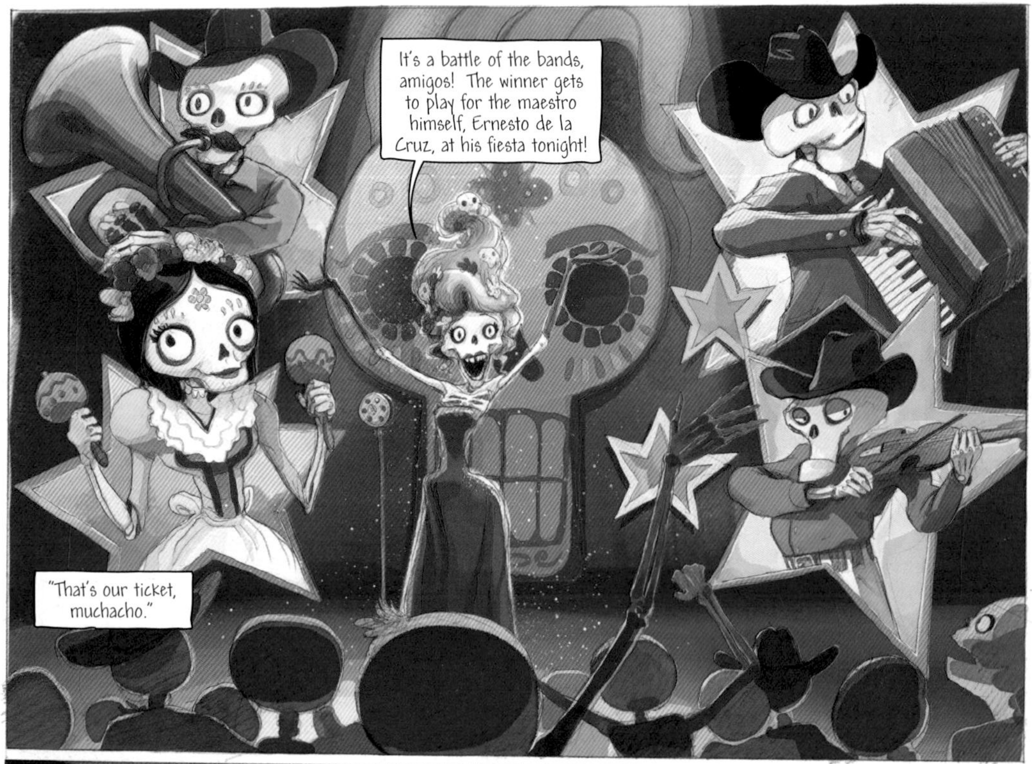
It's a battle of the bands, amigos! The winner gets to play for the maestro himself, Ernesto de la Cruz, at his fiesta tonight!
"That's our ticket, muchacho."

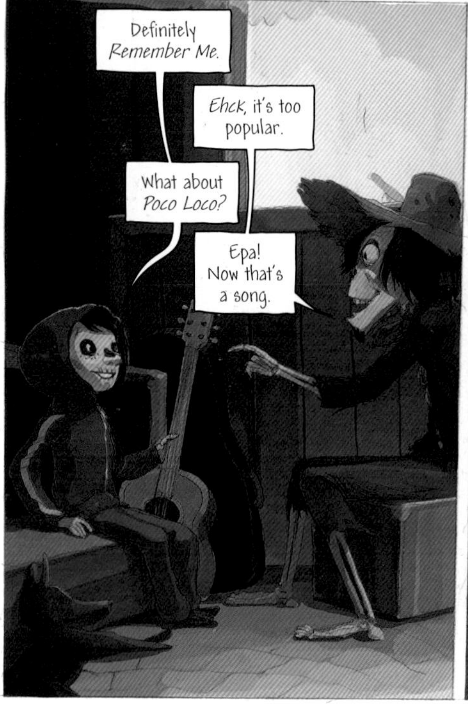
Definitely *Remember Me.*
Ehck, it's too popular.
What about *Poco Loco?*
Epa! Now that's a song.

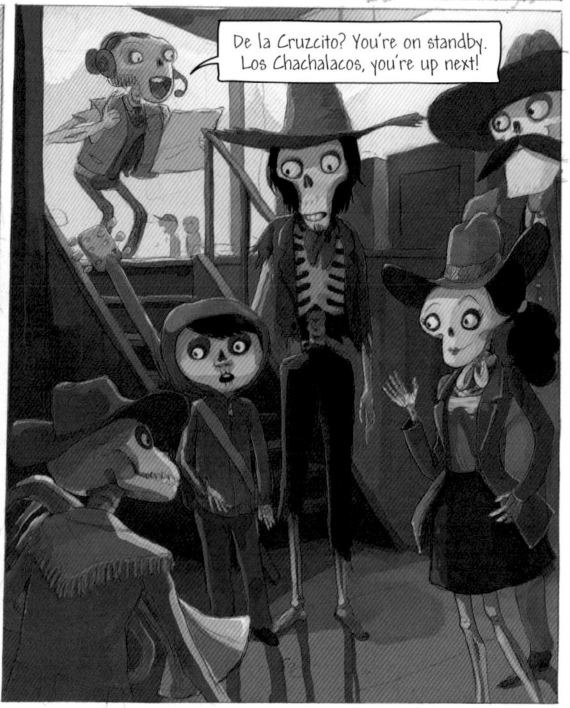
De la Cruzcito? You're on standby. Los Chachalacos, you're up next!

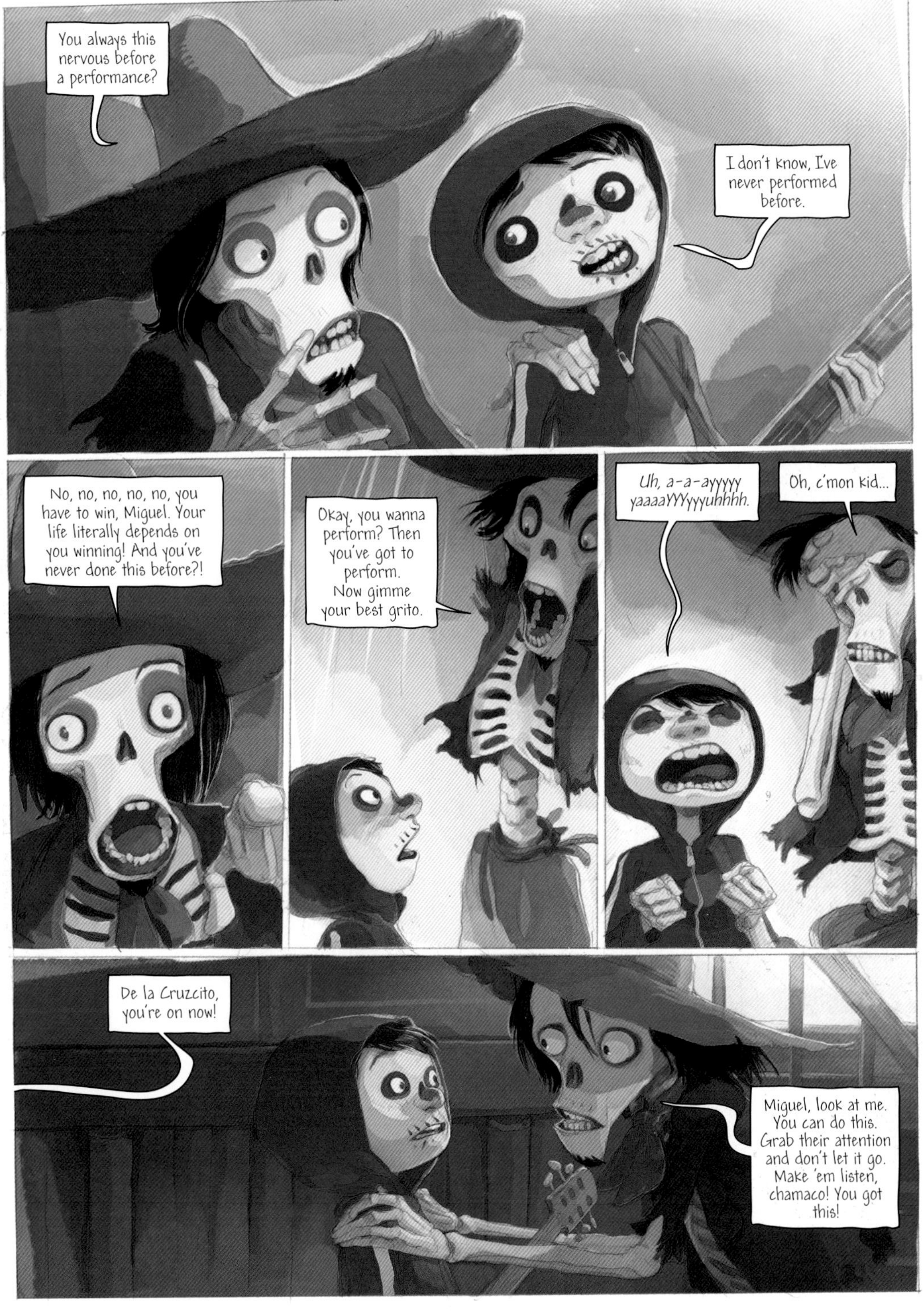
You always this nervous before a performance?
I don't know, I've never performed before.
No, no, no, no, no, you have to win, Miguel. Your life literally depends on you winning! And you've never done this before?!
Okay, you wanna perform? Then you've got to perform. Now gimme your best grito.
Uh, a-a-ayyyyy yaaaaYYYyyyuhhhh.
Oh, c'mon kid...
De la Cruzcito, you're on now!
Miguel, look at me. You can do this. Grab their attention and don't let it go. Make 'em listen, chamaco! You got this!

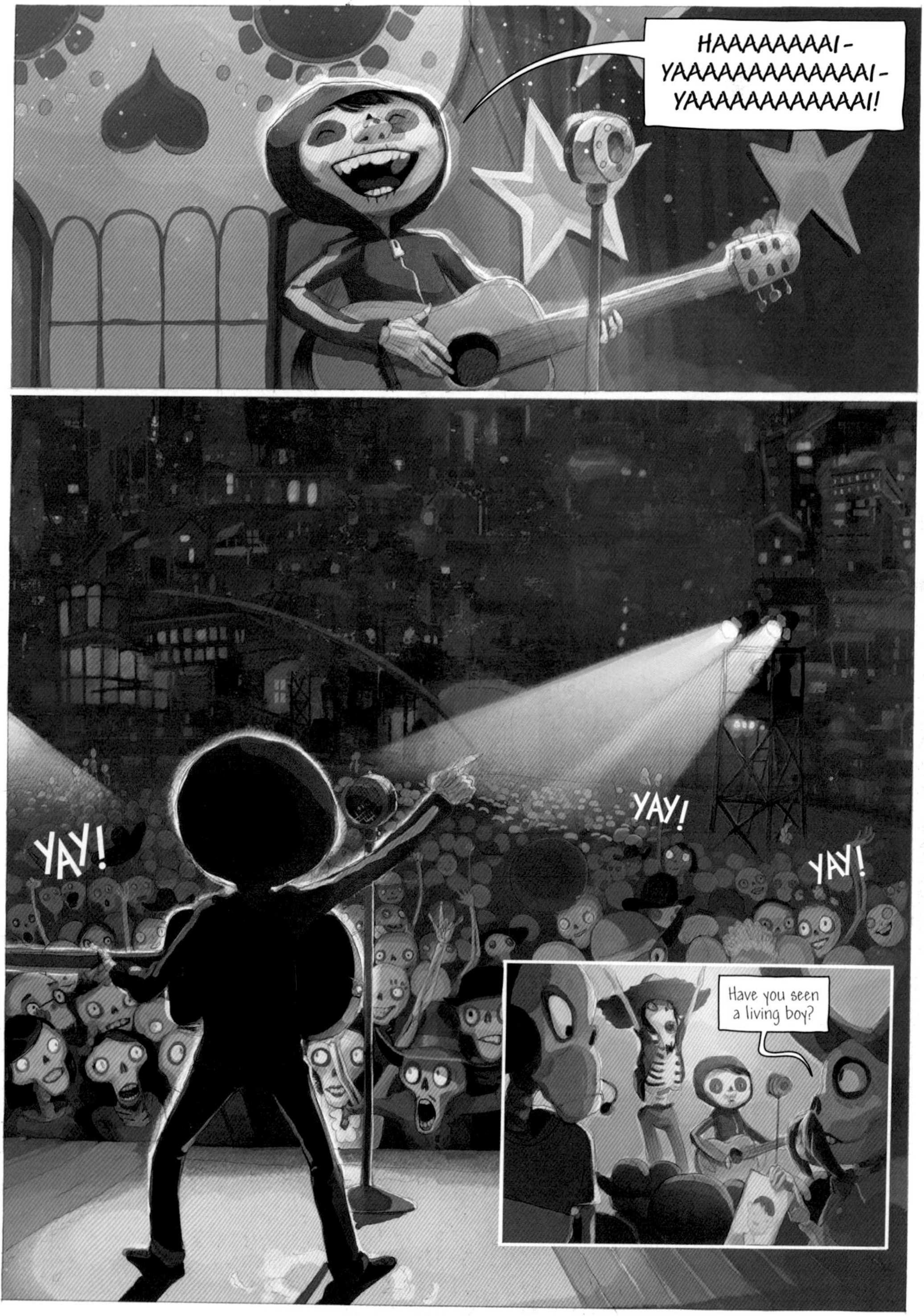
HAAAAAAAAI-
YAAAAAAAAAAAAAI-
YAAAAAAAAAAAAI!
YAY!
YAY!
YAY!
Have you seen
a living boy?

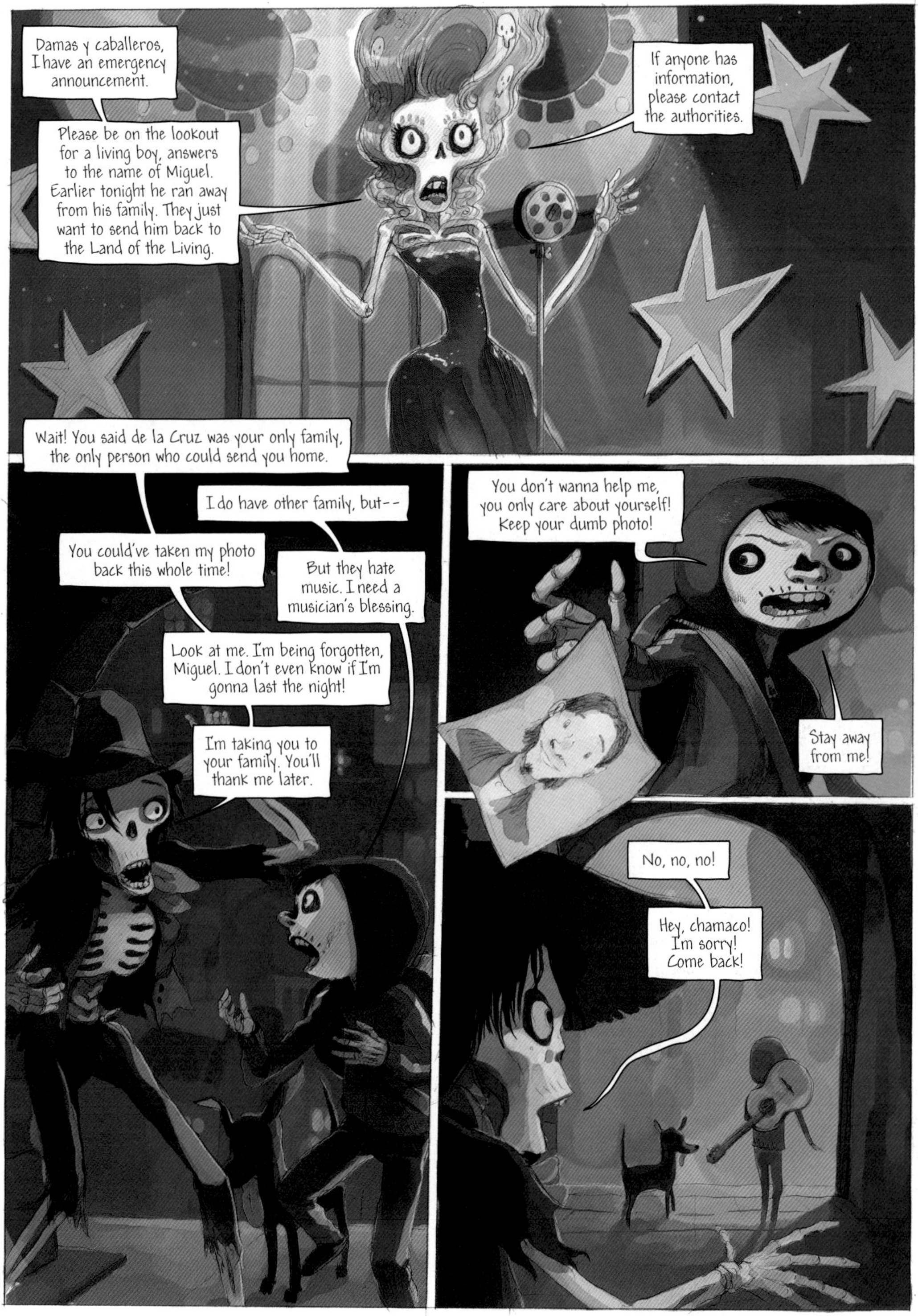
Damas y caballeros, I have an emergency announcement.
Please be on the lookout for a living boy, answers to the name of Miguel. Earlier tonight he ran away from his family. They just want to send him back to the Land of the Living.
If anyone has information, please contact the authorities.
Wait! You said de la Cruz was your only family, the only person who could send you home.
I do have other family, but--
You could've taken my photo back this whole time!
But they hate music. I need a musician's blessing.
Look at me. I'm being forgotten, Miguel. I don't even know if I'm gonna last the night!
I'm taking you to your family. You'll thank me later.
You don't wanna help me, you only care about yourself! Keep your dumb photo!
Stay away from me!
No, no, no!
Hey, chamaco! I'm sorry! Come back!

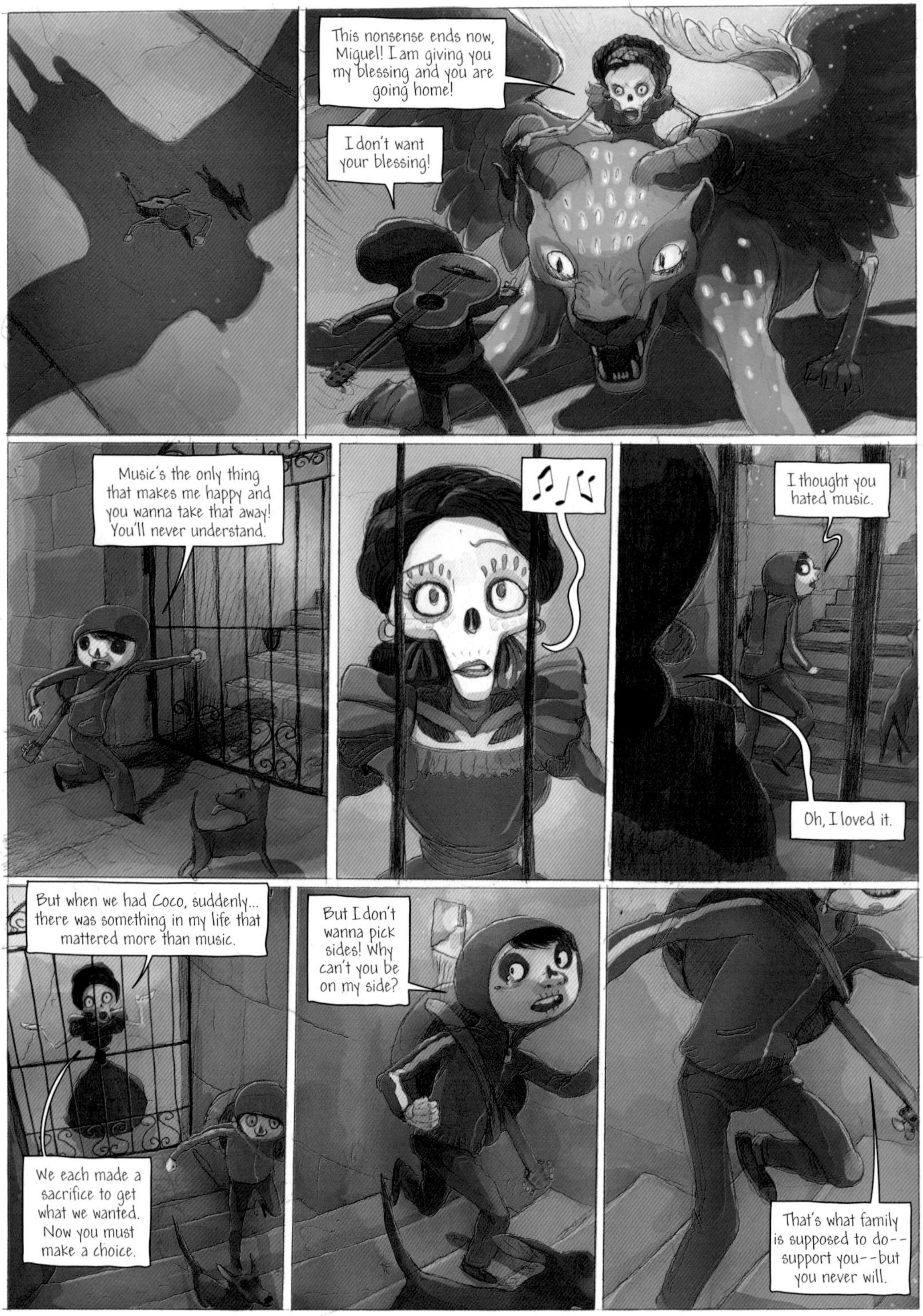
This nonsense ends now, Miguel! I am giving you my blessing and you are going home!
I don't want your blessing!
Music's the only thing that makes me happy and you wanna take that away! You'll never understand.
I thought you hated music.
Oh, I loved it.
But when we had Coco, suddenly... there was something in my life that mattered more than music.
We each made a sacrifice to get what we wanted. Now you must make a choice.
But I don't wanna pick sides! Why can't you be on my side?
That's what family is supposed to do--support you--but you never will.

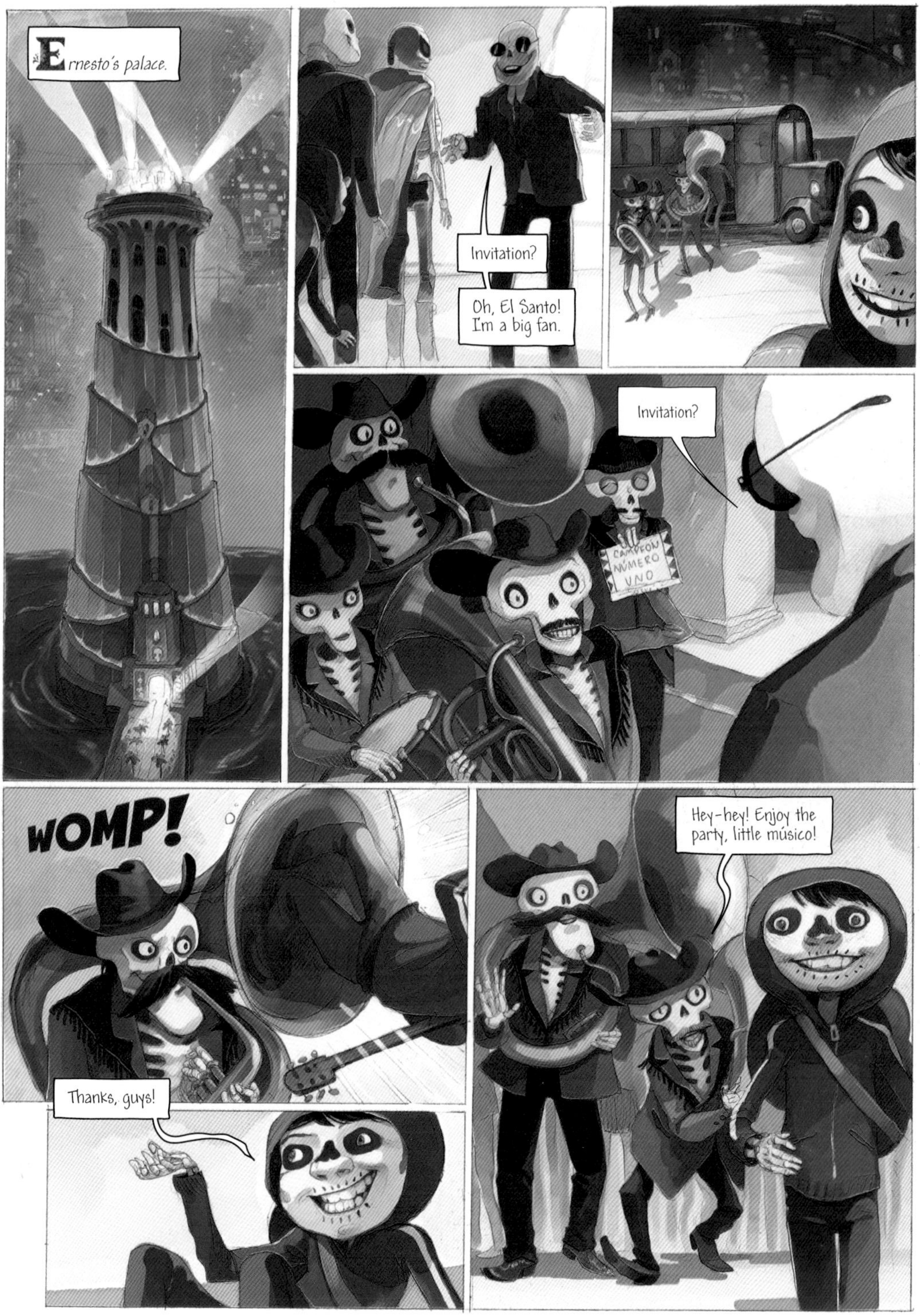
Ernesto's palace.
Invitation?
Oh, El Santo! I'm a big fan.
Invitation?
CAMPEON NÚMERO UNO
WOMP!
Thanks, guys!
Hey-hey! Enjoy the party, little músico!

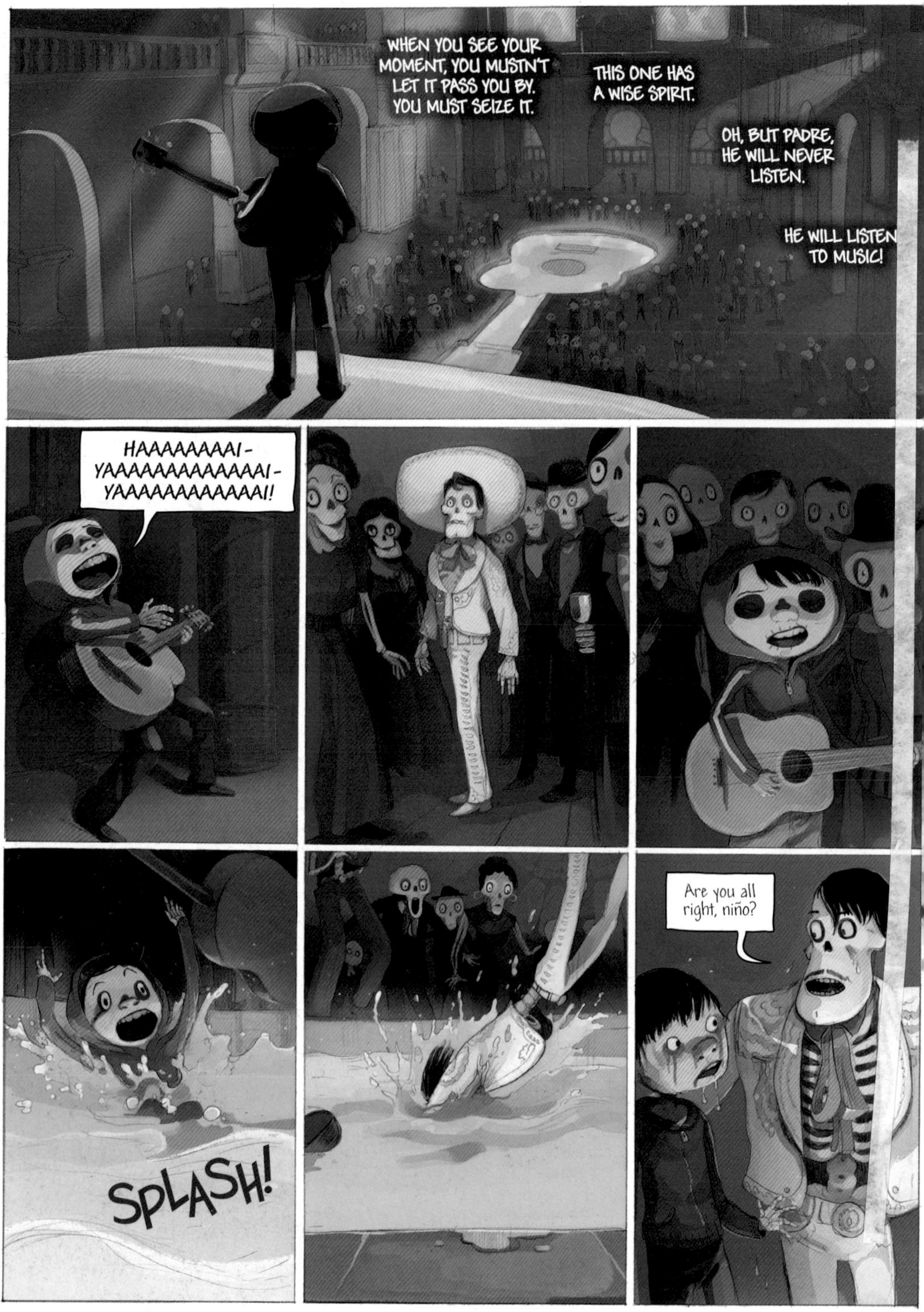
WHEN YOU SEE YOUR MOMENT, YOU MUSTN'T LET IT PASS YOU BY. YOU MUST SEIZE IT.
THIS ONE HAS A WISE SPIRIT.
OH, BUT PADRE, HE WILL NEVER LISTEN.
HE WILL LISTEN TO MUSIC!
HAAAAAAAAI-YAAAAAAAAAAAAAI-YAAAAAAAAAAAAI!
SPLASH!
Are you all right, niño?

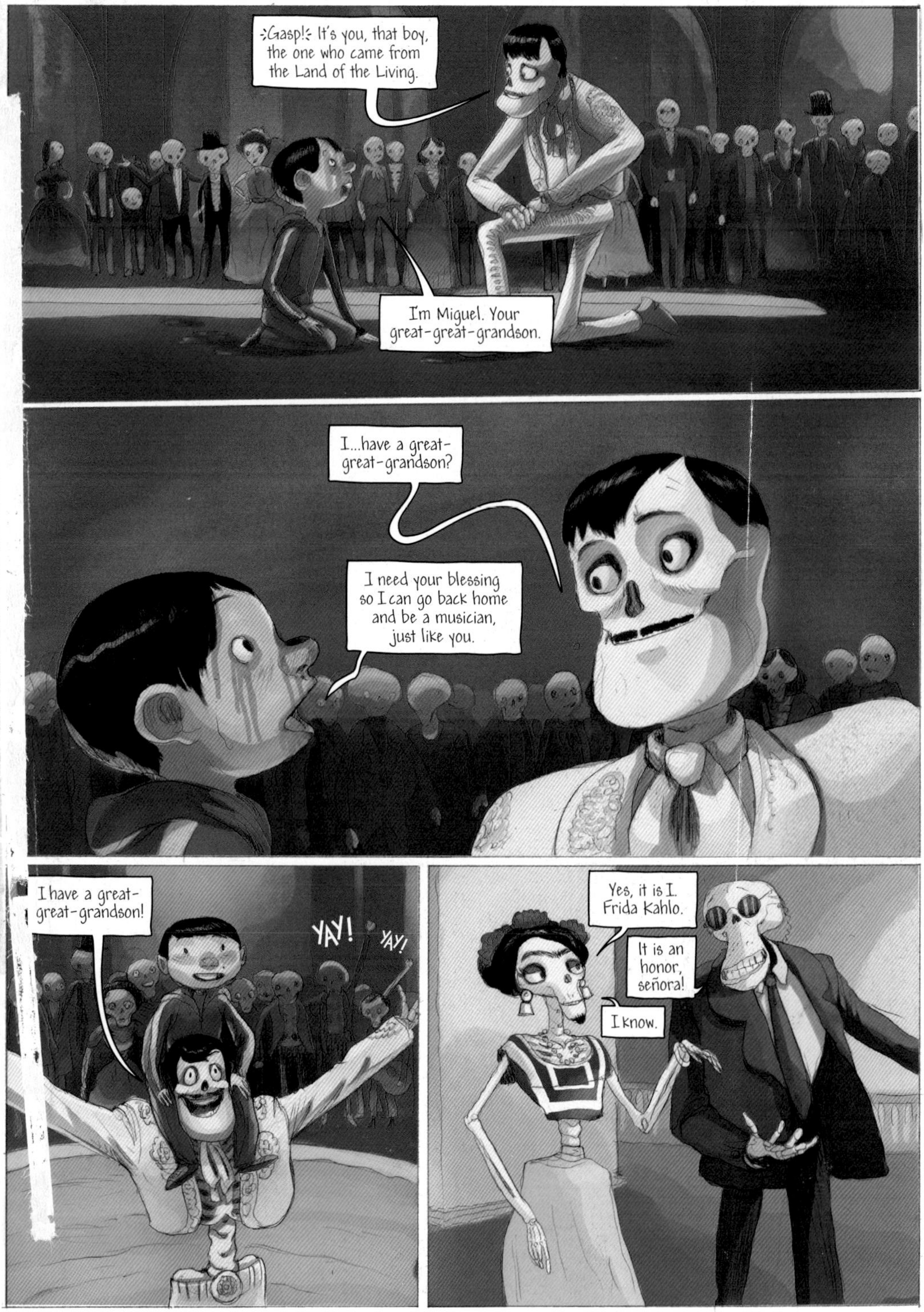
Gasp! It's you, that boy, the one who came from the Land of the Living.
I'm Miguel. Your great-great-grandson.
I...have a great-great-grandson?
I need your blessing so I can go back home and be a musician, just like you.
I have a great-great-grandson!
YAY!
YAY!
Yes, it is I. Frida Kahlo.
It is an honor, señora!
I know.

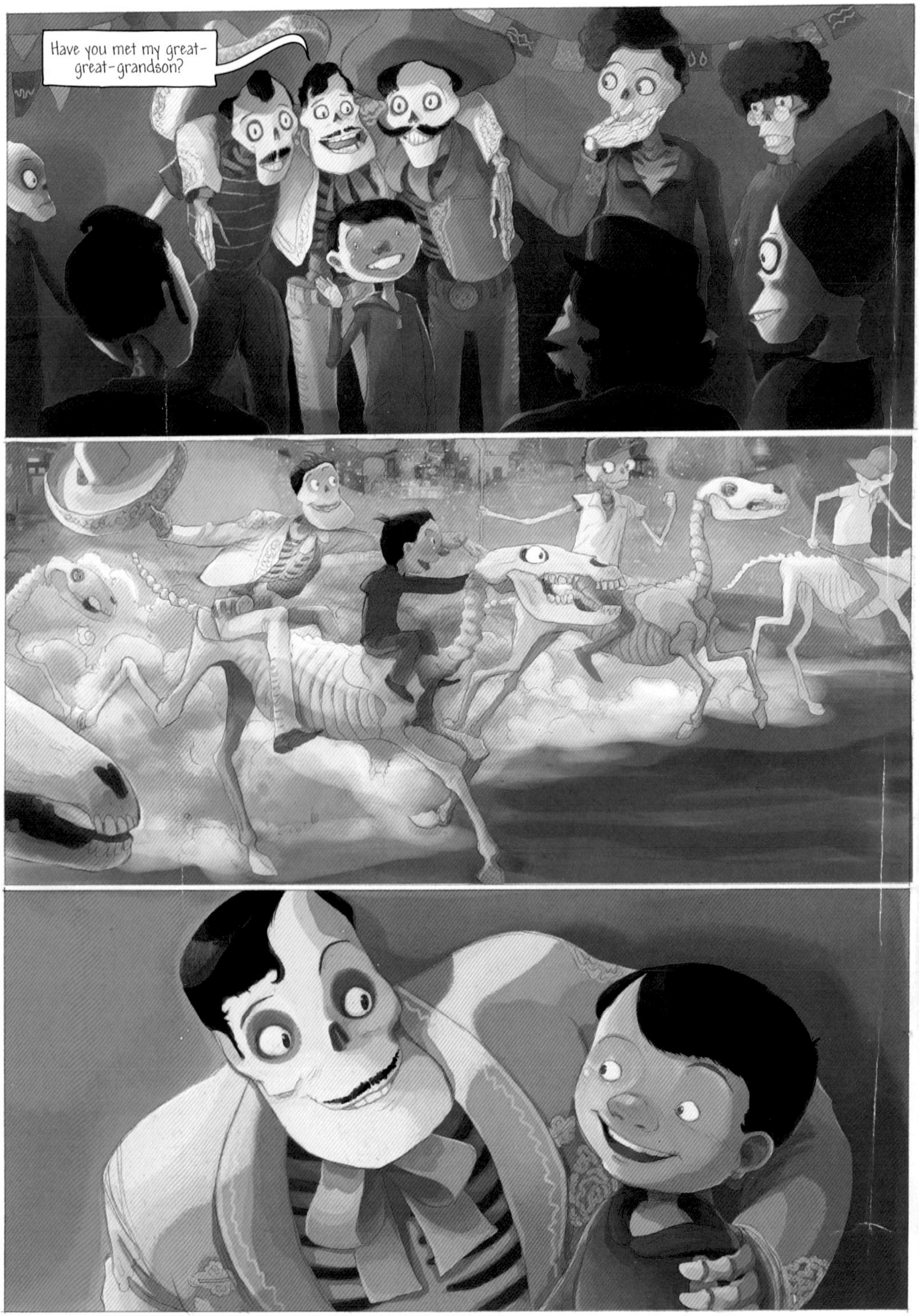
Have you met my great-great-grandson?

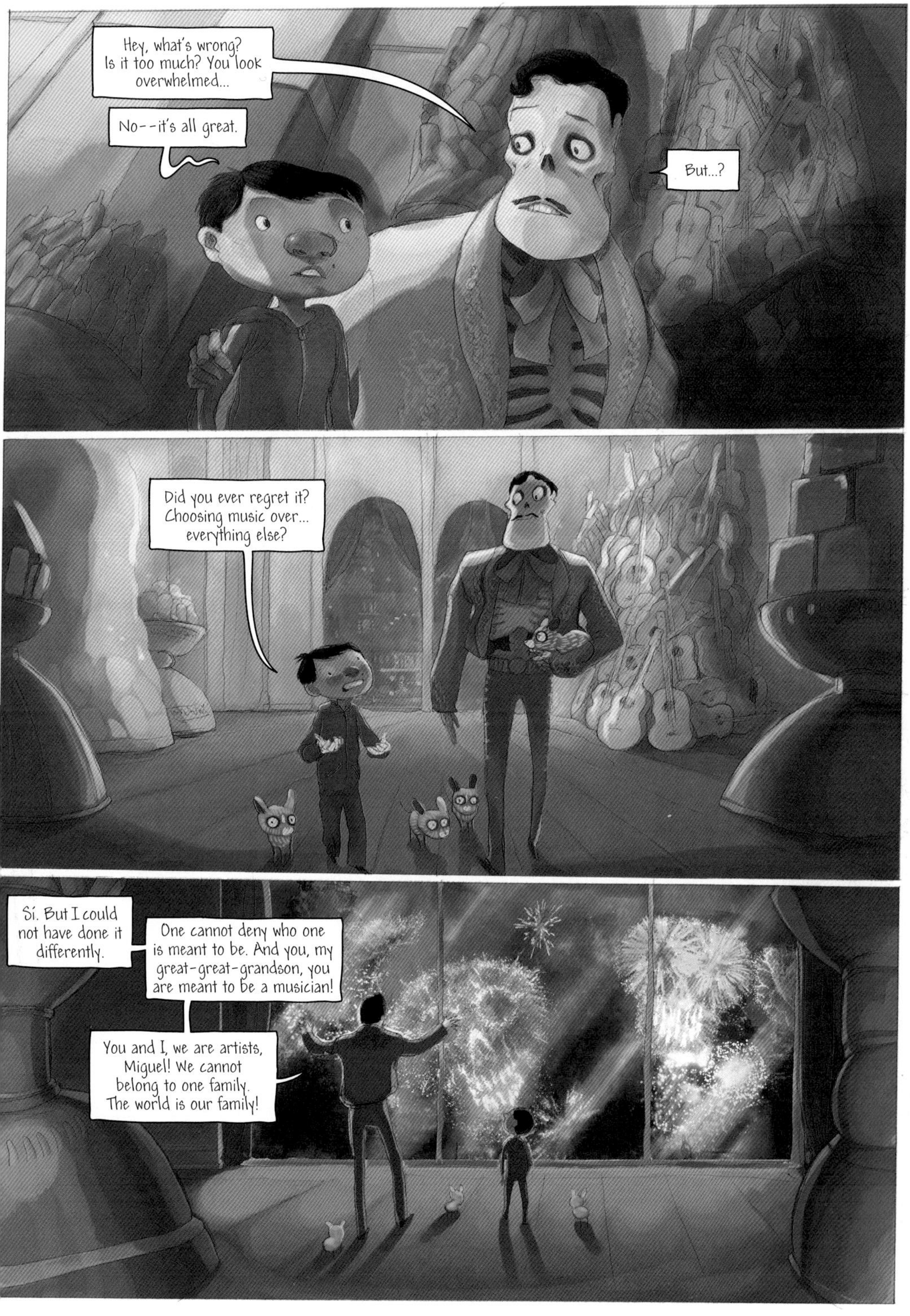
Hey, what's wrong? Is it too much? You look overwhelmed...
No--it's all great.
But...?
Did you ever regret it? Choosing music over... everything else?
Sí. But I could not have done it differently.
One cannot deny who one is meant to be. And you, my great-great-grandson, you are meant to be a musician!
You and I, we are artists, Miguel! We cannot belong to one family. The world is our family!

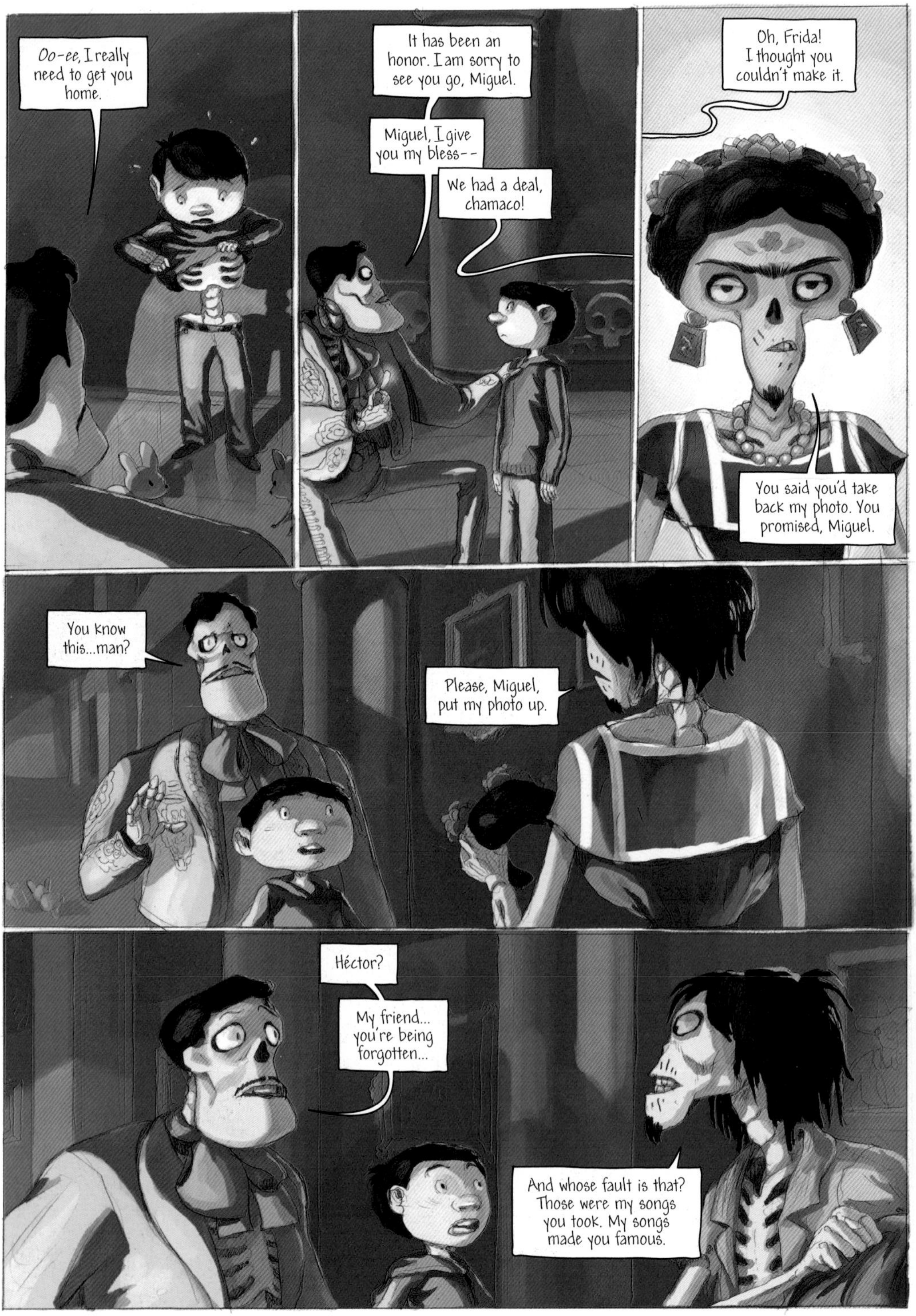
Oo-ee, I really need to get you home.
It has been an honor. I am sorry to see you go, Miguel.
Miguel, I give you my bless--
We had a deal, chamaco!
Oh, Frida! I thought you couldn't make it.
You said you'd take back my photo. You promised, Miguel.
You know this...man?
Please, Miguel, put my photo up.
Héctor?
My friend... you're being forgotten...
And whose fault is that? Those were my songs you took. My songs made you famous.

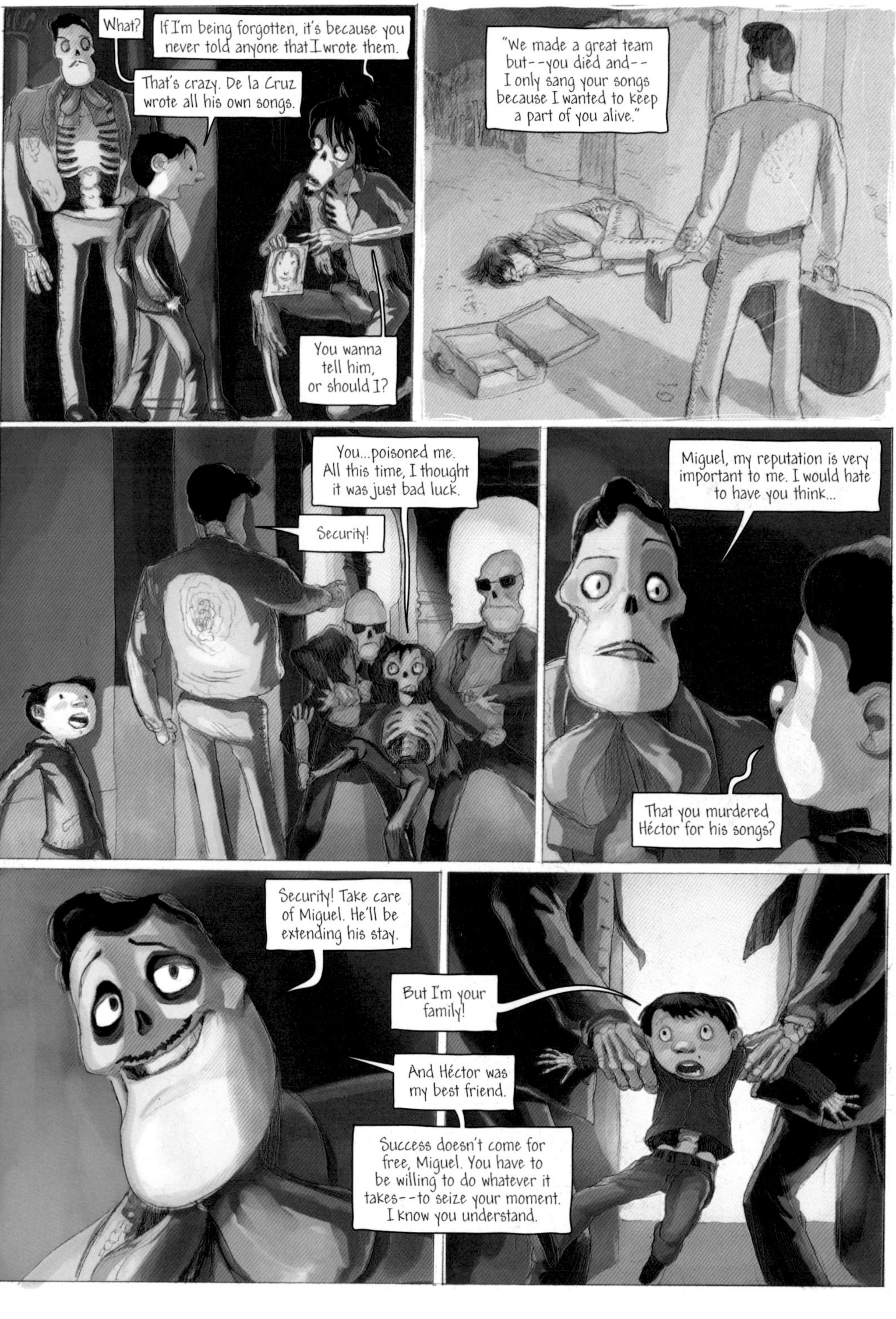
What?
If I'm being forgotten, it's because you never told anyone that I wrote them.
That's crazy. De la Cruz wrote all his own songs.
You wanna tell him, or should I?
"We made a great team but--you died and--I only sang your songs because I wanted to keep a part of you alive."
You...poisoned me. All this time, I thought it was just bad luck.
Security!
Miguel, my reputation is very important to me. I would hate to have you think...
That you murdered Héctor for his songs?
Security! Take care of Miguel. He'll be extending his stay.
But I'm your family!
And Héctor was my best friend.
Success doesn't come for free, Miguel. You have to be willing to do whatever it takes--to seize your moment. I know you understand.

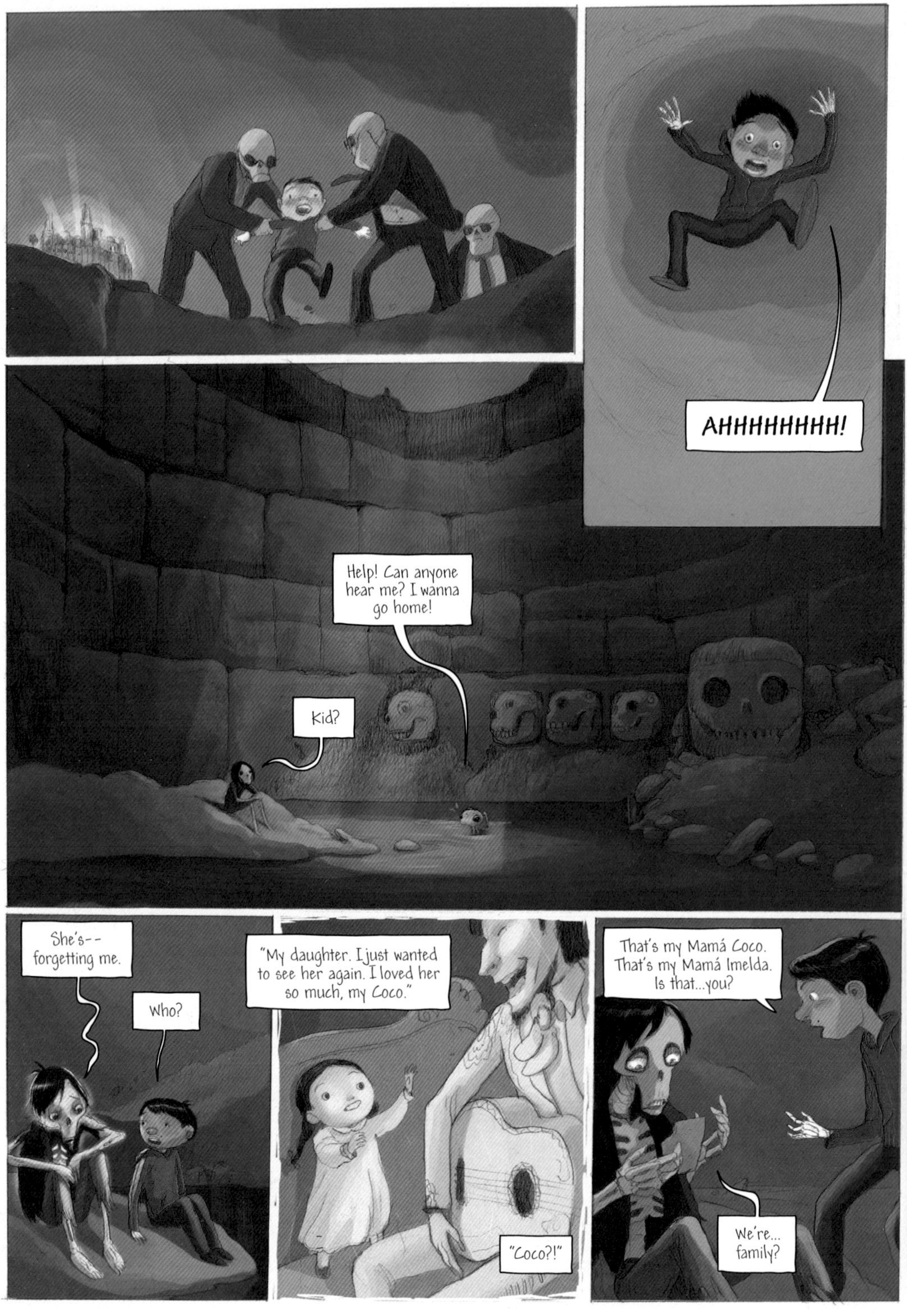
AHHHHHHHH!
Help! Can anyone hear me? I wanna go home!
Kid?
She's-- forgetting me.
Who?
"My daughter. I just wanted to see her again. I loved her so much, my Coco."
"Coco?!"
That's my Mamá Coco. That's my Mamá Imelda. Is that...you?
We're... family?

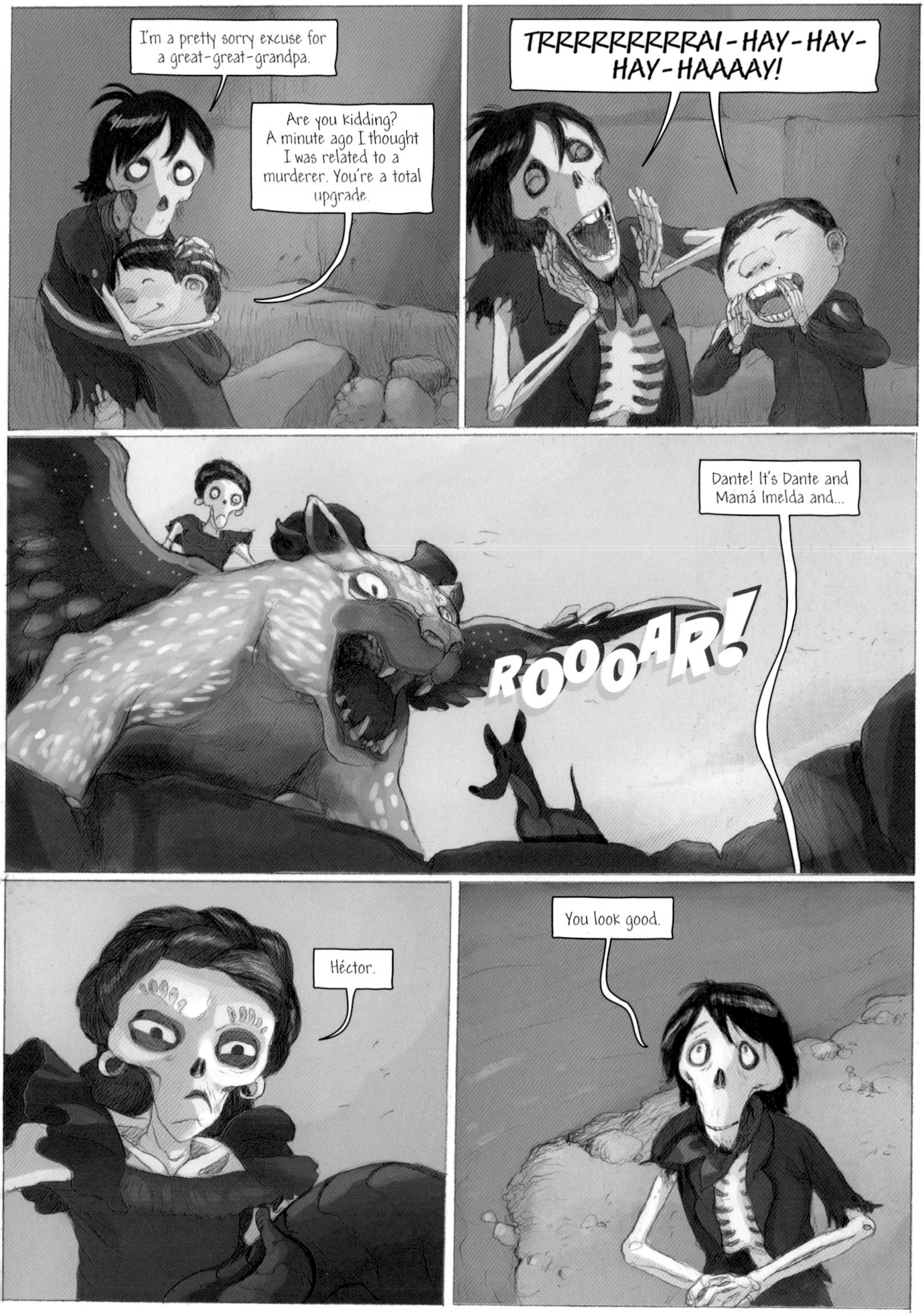
I'm a pretty sorry excuse for a great-great-grandpa.
Are you kidding? A minute ago I thought I was related to a murderer. You're a total upgrade.
TRRRRRRRRRRAI-HAY-HAY-HAY-HAAAAY!
Dante! It's Dante and Mamá Imelda and...
ROOOAR!
Héctor.
You look good.

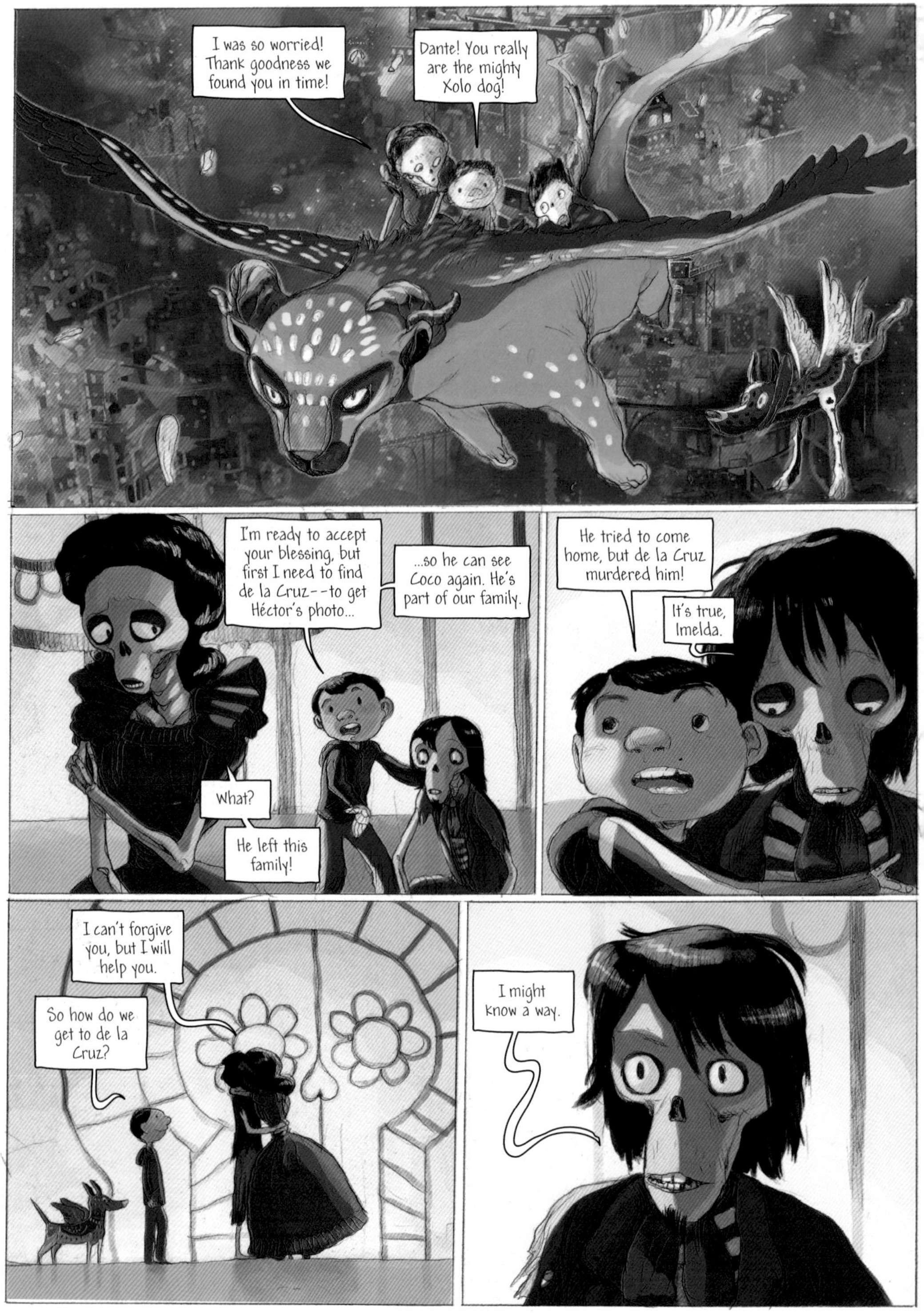
I was so worried! Thank goodness we found you in time!
Dante! You really are the mighty Xolo dog!
I'm ready to accept your blessing, but first I need to find de la Cruz--to get Héctor's photo...
...so he can see Coco again. He's part of our family.
What?
He left this family!
He tried to come home, but de la Cruz murdered him!
It's true, Imelda.
I can't forgive you, but I will help you.
So how do we get to de la Cruz?
I might know a way.

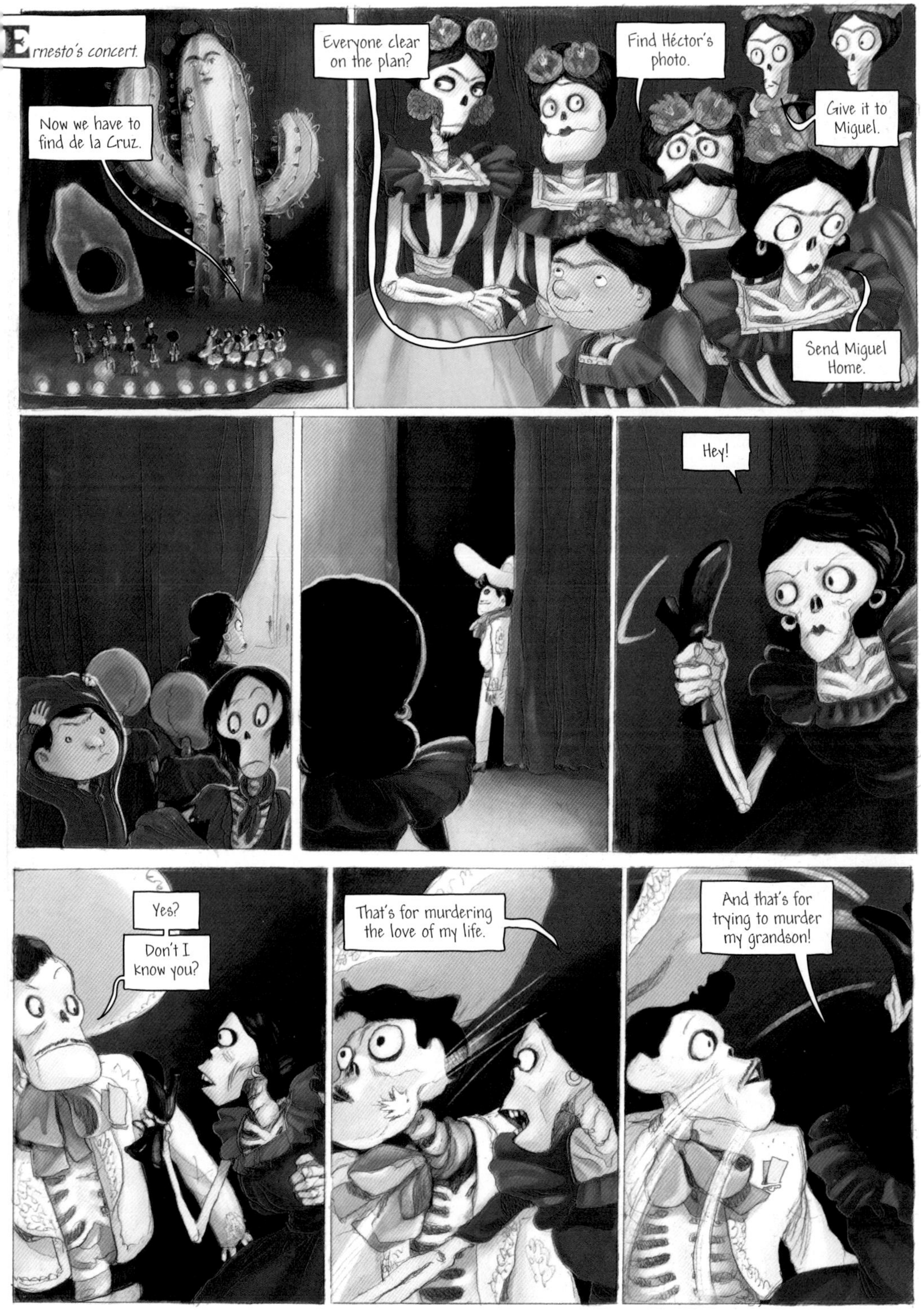
Ernesto's concert.
Now we have to find de la Cruz.
Everyone clear on the plan?
Find Héctor's photo.
Give it to Miguel.
Send Miguel Home.
Hey!
Yes?
Don't I know you?
That's for murdering the love of my life.
And that's for trying to murder my grandson!

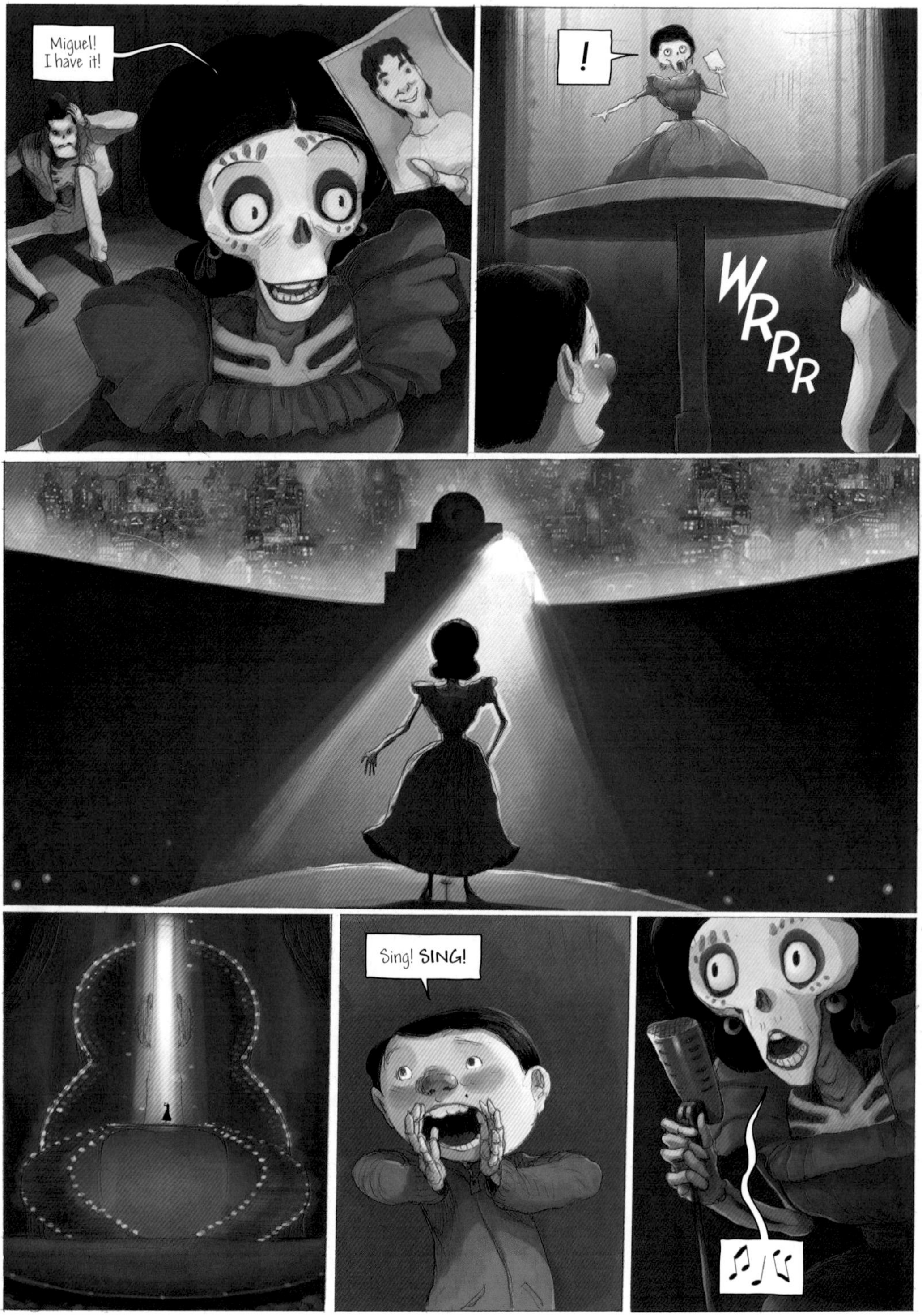
Miguel! I have it!
!
WRRRR
Sing! SING!

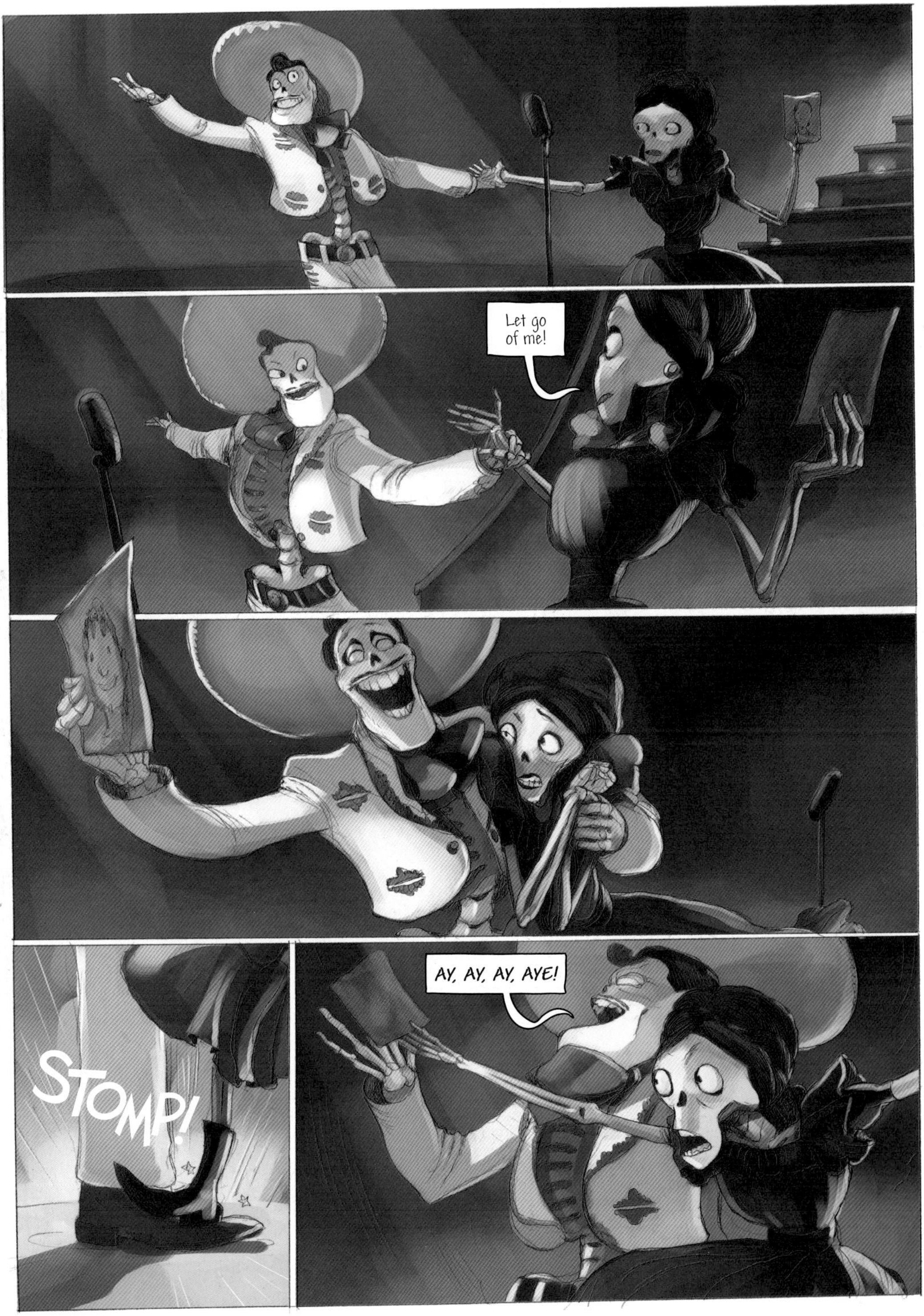
Let go of me!
STOMP!
AY, AY, AY, AYE!

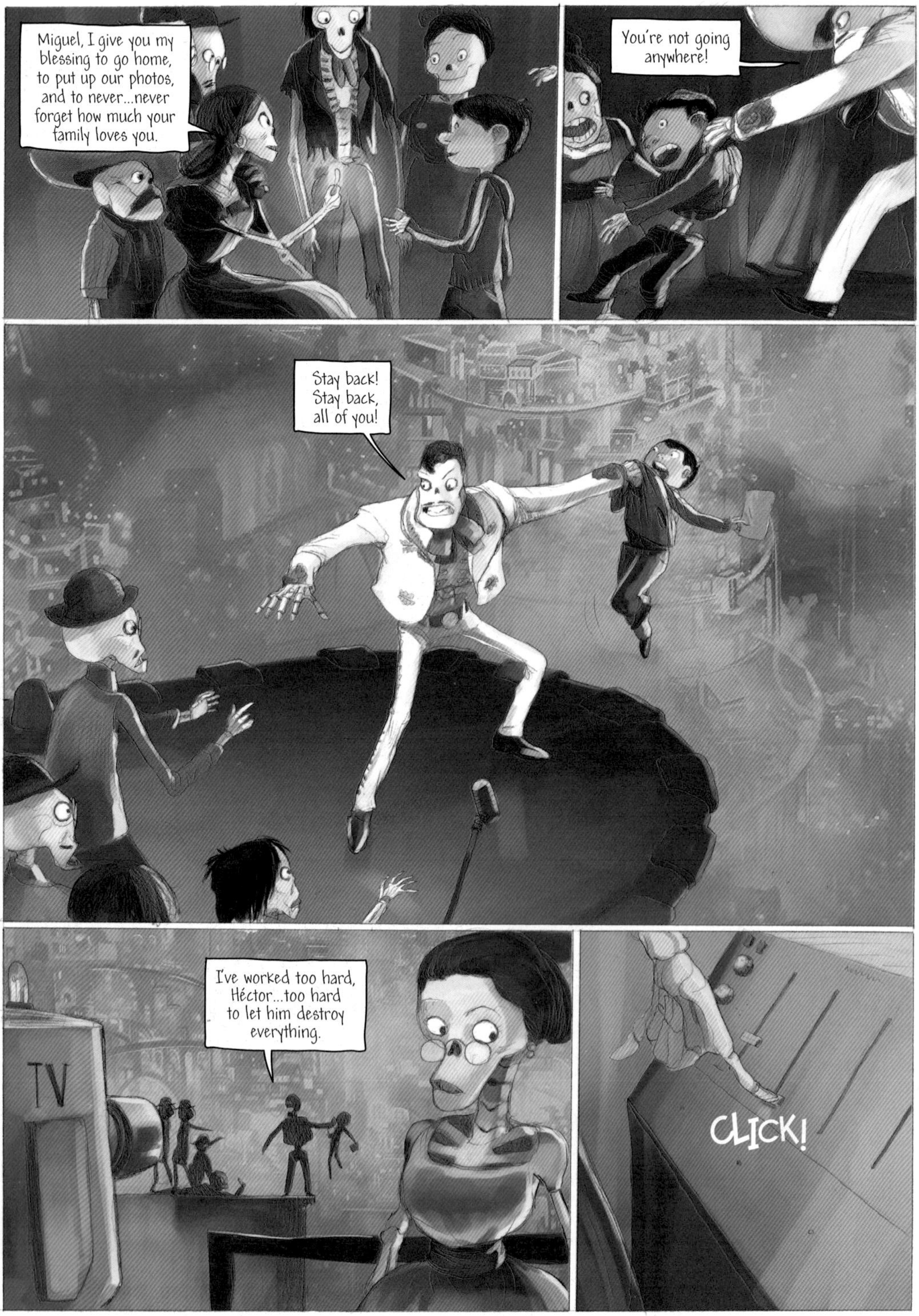
Miguel, I give you my blessing to go home, to put up our photos, and to never...never forget how much your family loves you.
You're not going anywhere!
Stay back! Stay back, all of you!
I've worked too hard, Héctor...too hard to let him destroy everything.
TV
CLICK!

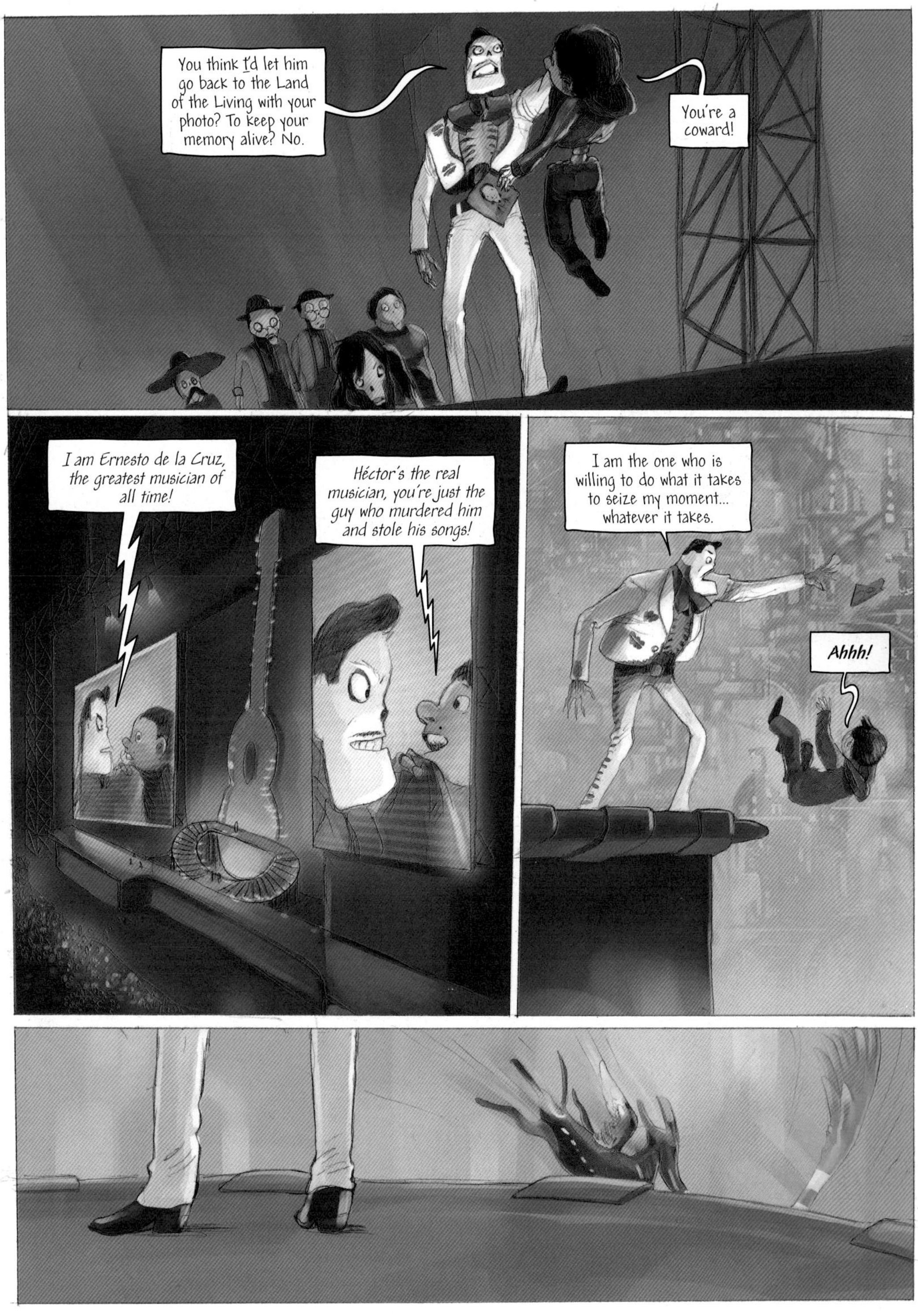
You think I'd let him go back to the Land of the Living with your photo? To keep your memory alive? No.
You're a coward!
I am Ernesto de la Cruz, the greatest musician of all time!
Héctor's the real musician, you're just the guy who murdered him and stole his songs!
I am the one who is willing to do what it takes to seize my moment... whatever it takes.
Ahhh!

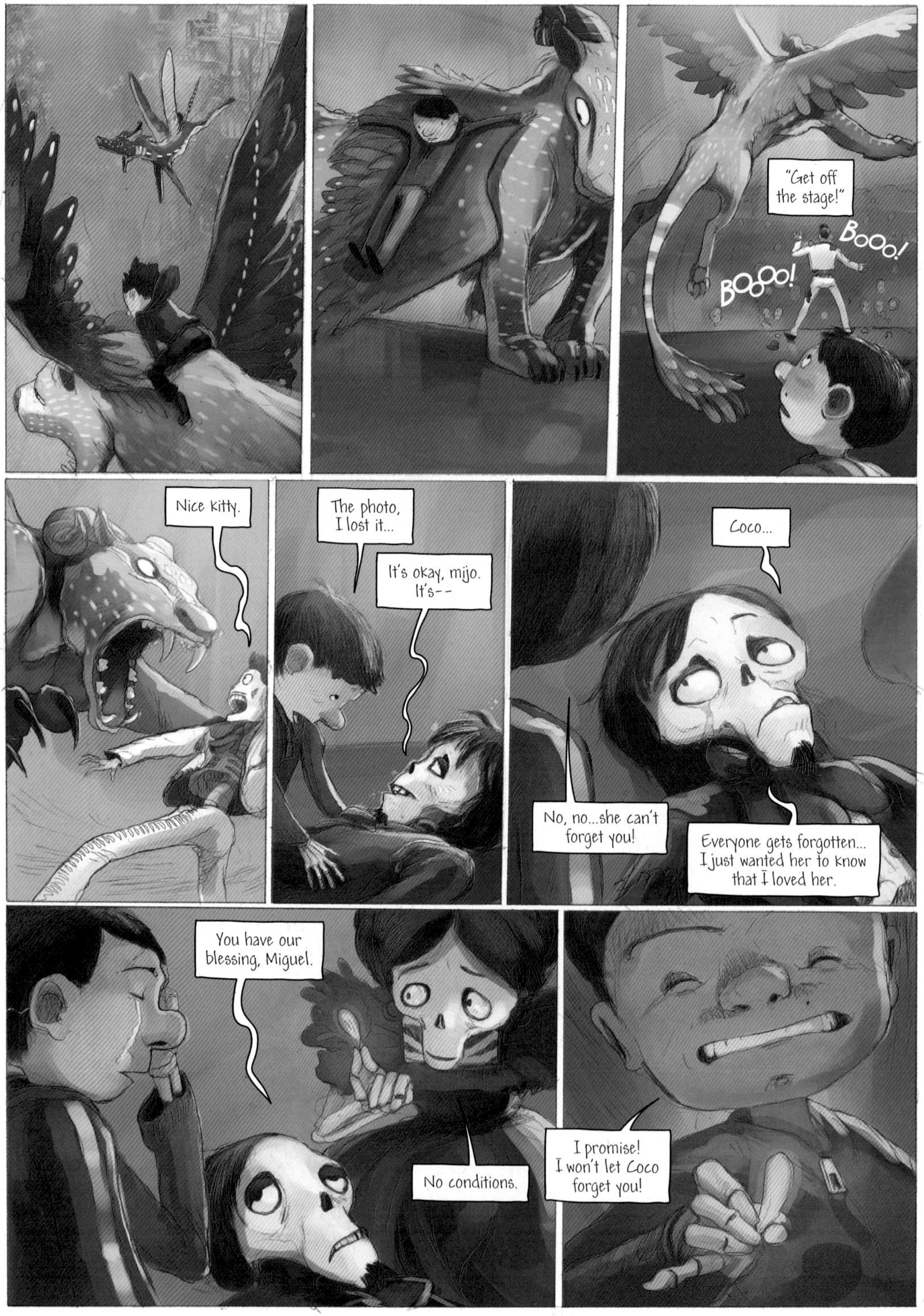
"Get off the stage!"
BOOOO!
BOOOO!
Nice kitty.
The photo, I lost it...
It's okay, mijo. It's--
Coco...
No, no...she can't forget you!
Everyone gets forgotten... I just wanted her to know that I loved her.
You have our blessing, Miguel.
No conditions.
I promise! I won't let Coco forget you!

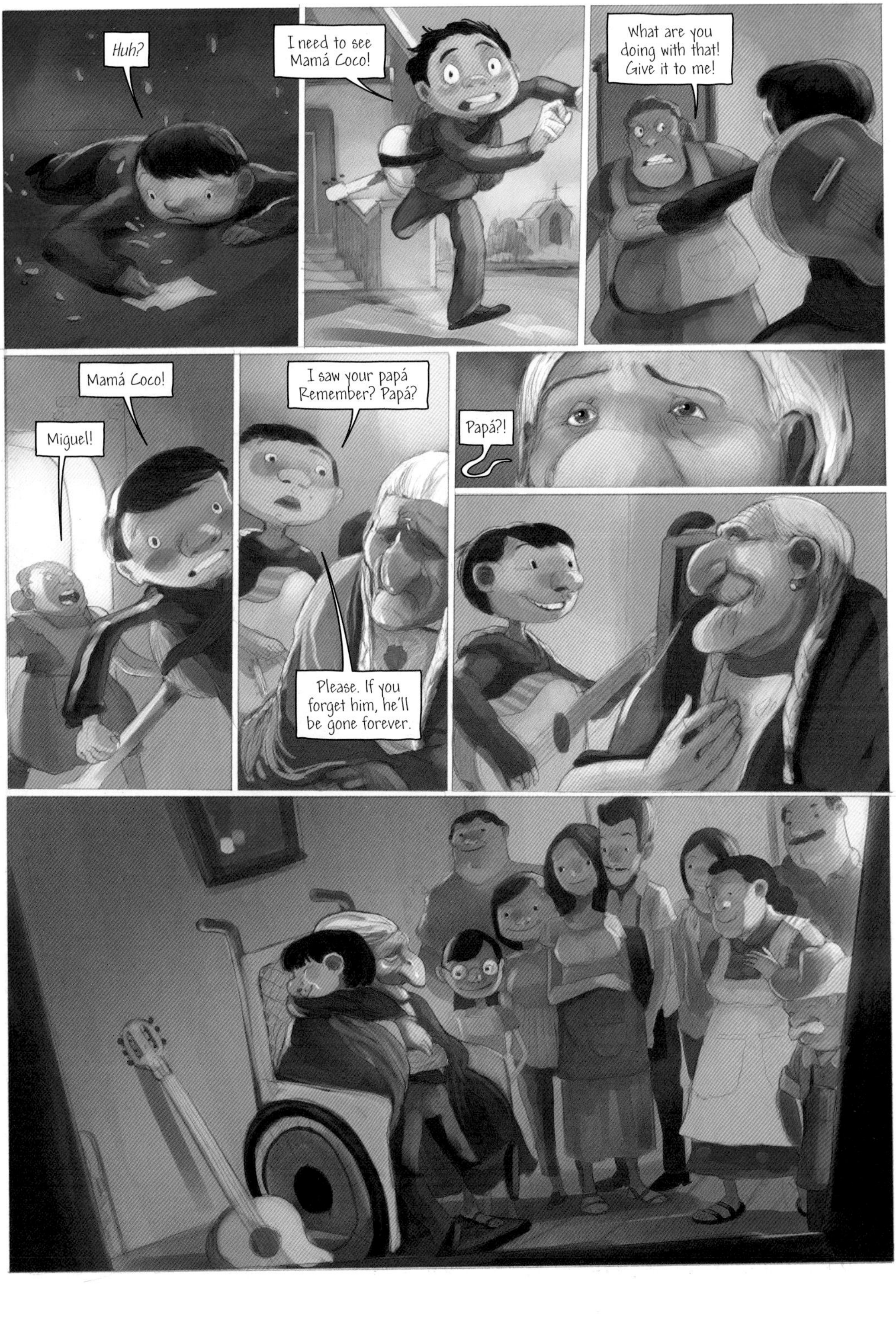
Huh?
I need to see Mamá Coco!
What are you doing with that! Give it to me!
Mamá Coco!
Miguel!
I saw your papá Remember? Papá?
Please. If you forget him, he'll be gone forever.
Papá?!

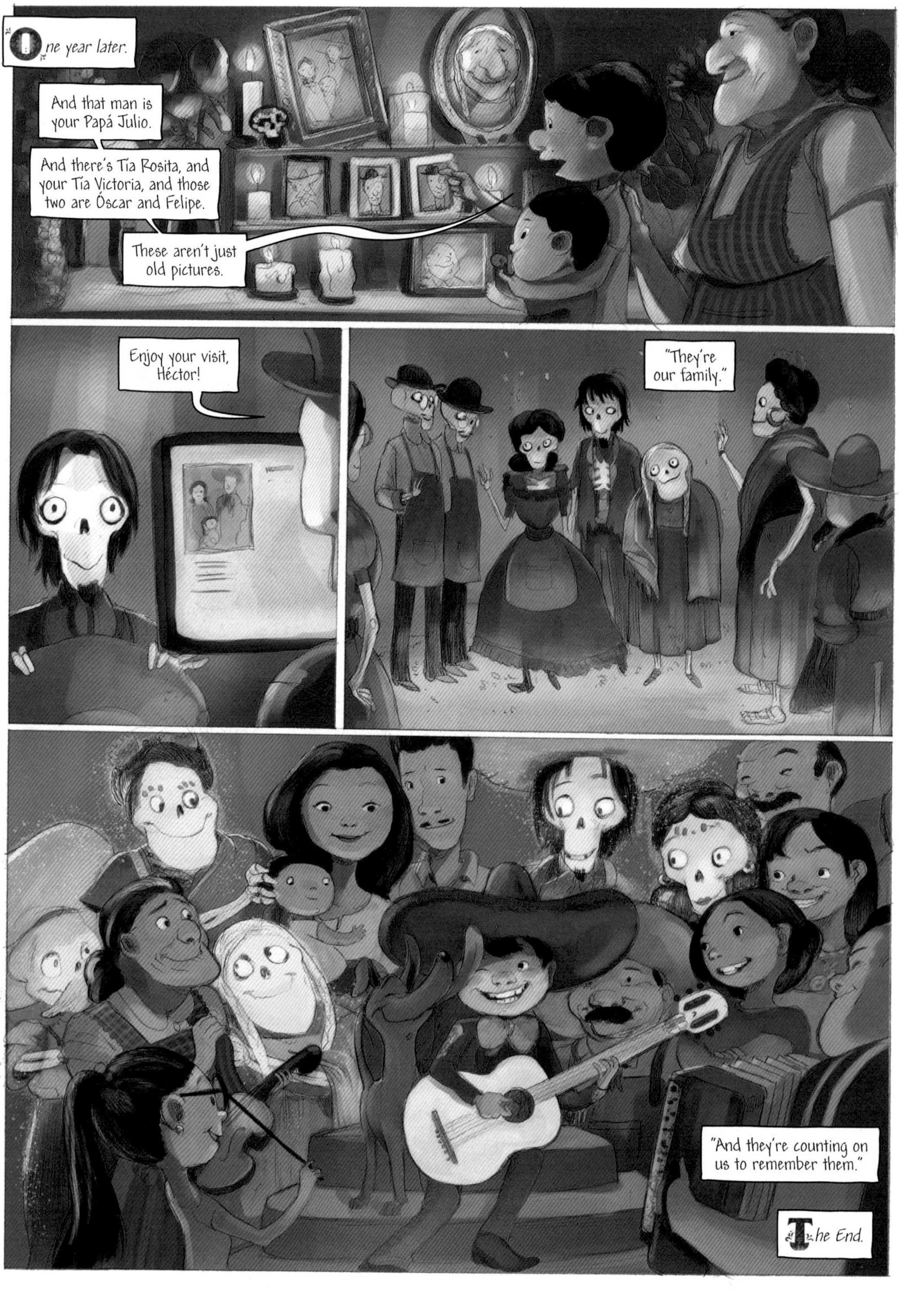
One year later.
And that man is your Papá Julio.
And there's Tía Rosita, and your Tía Victoria, and those two are Óscar and Felipe.
These aren't just old pictures.
Enjoy your visit, Héctor!
"They're our family."
"And they're counting on us to remember them."
The End.

"MUSIC'S THE ONLY THING THAT MAKES ME HAPPY."

-MIGUEL

The Making of the Graphic Novel

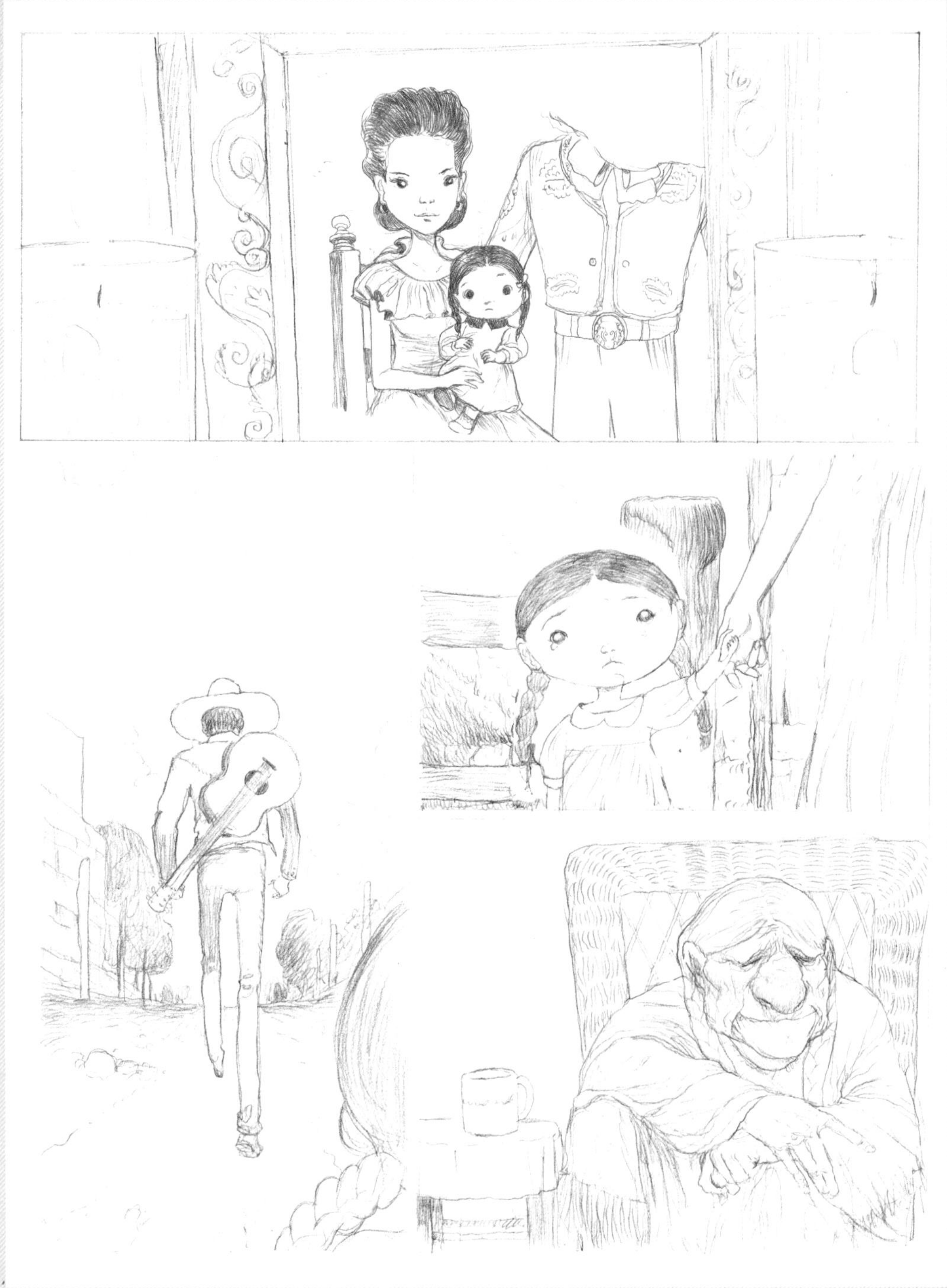

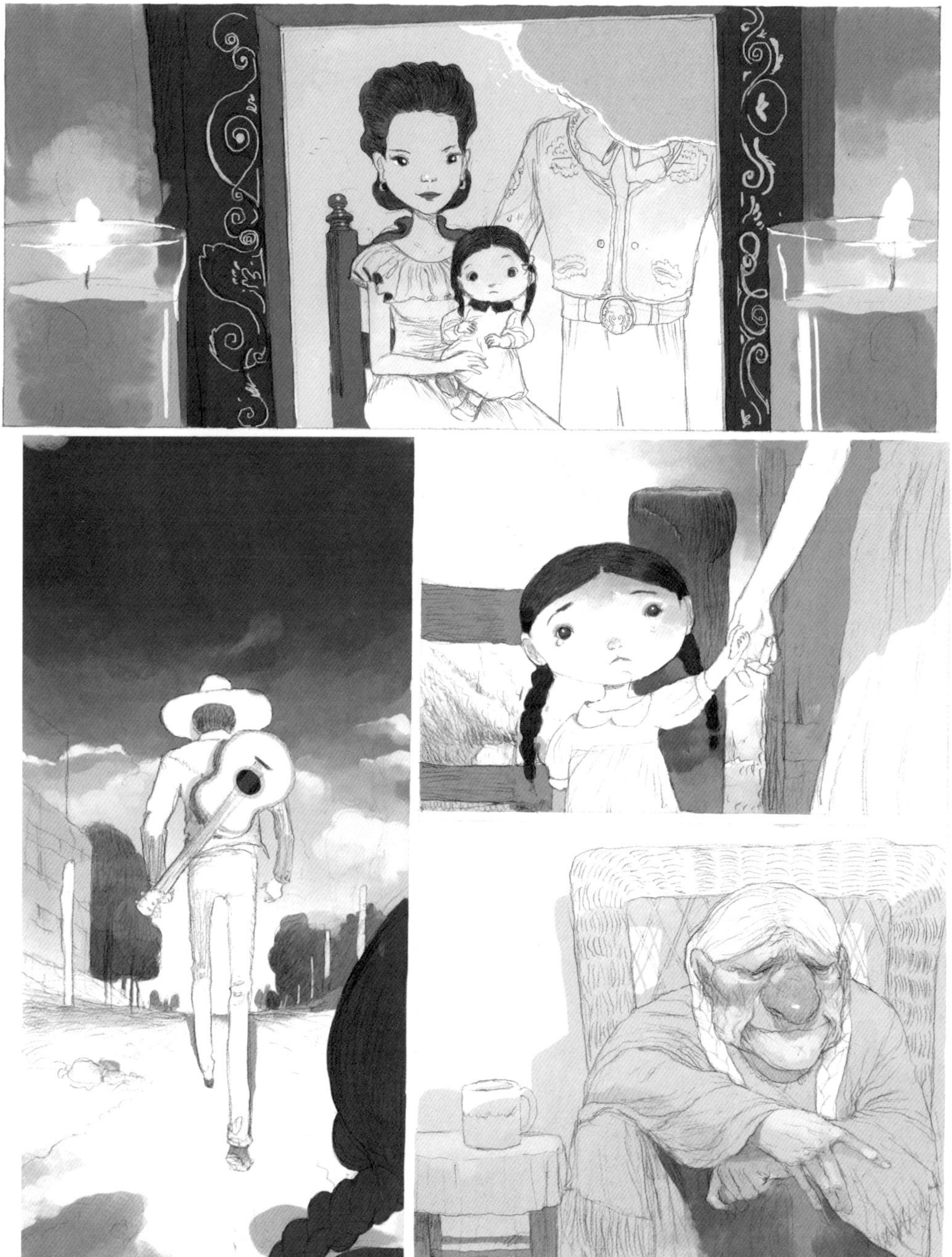

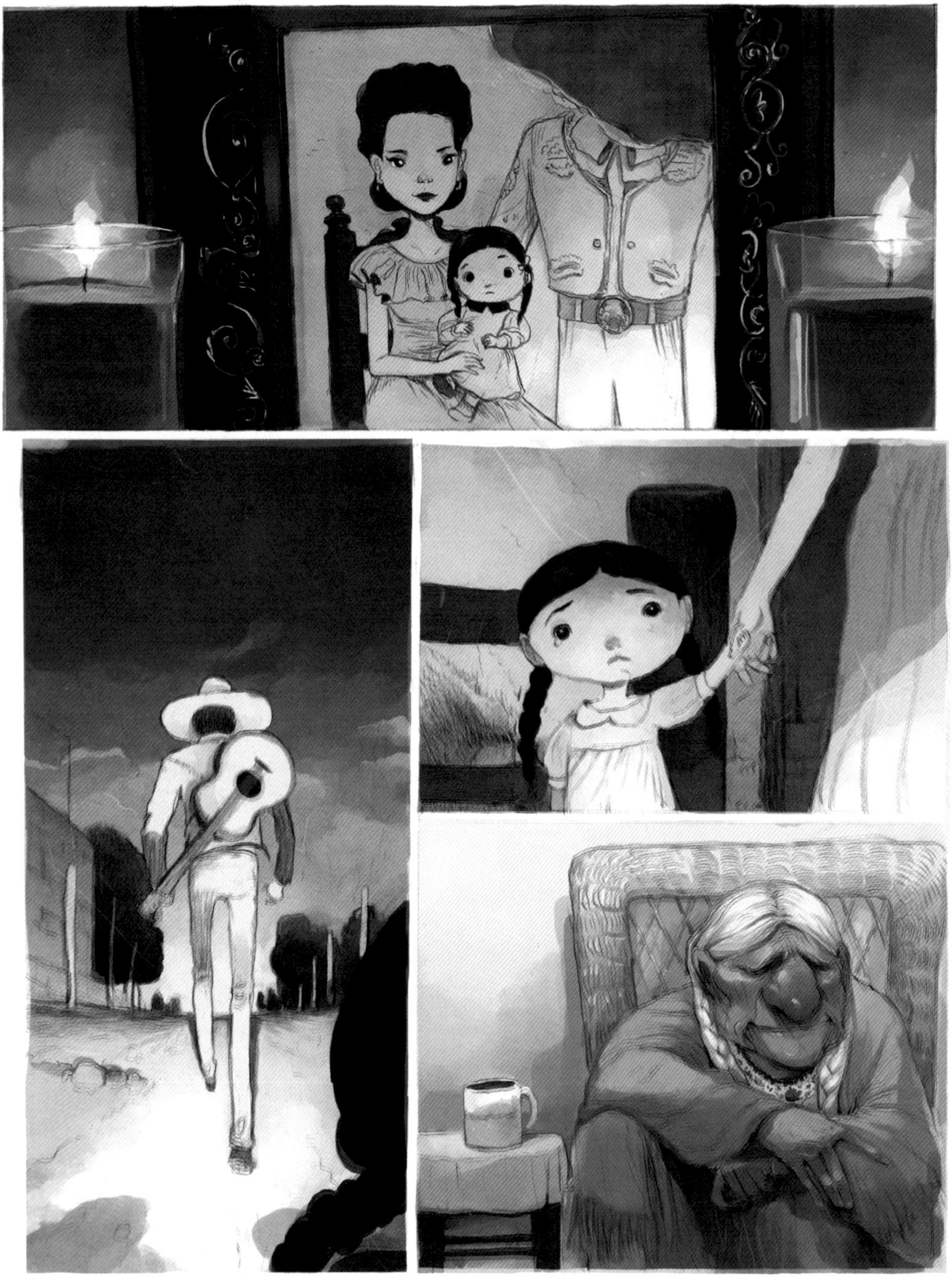

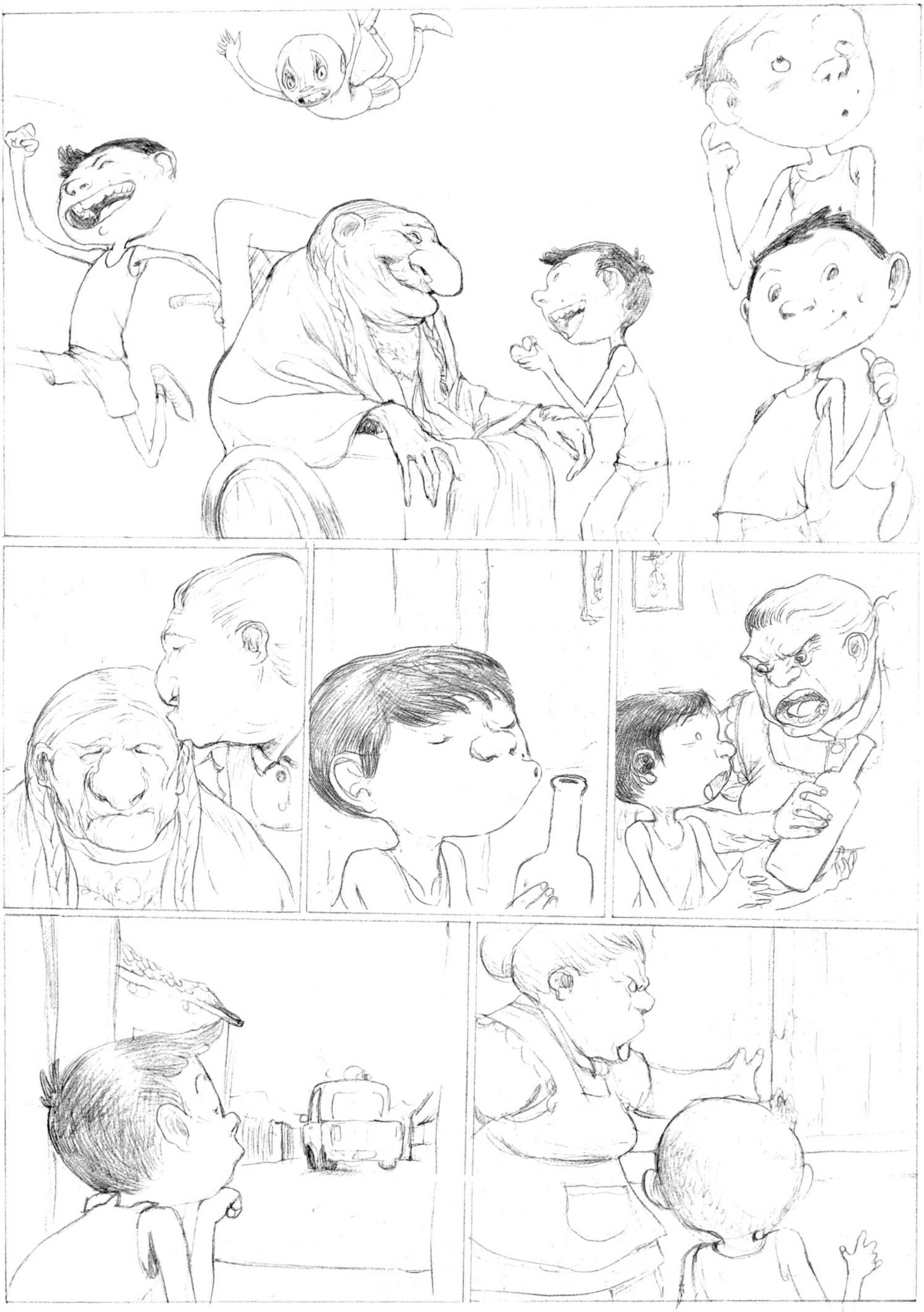

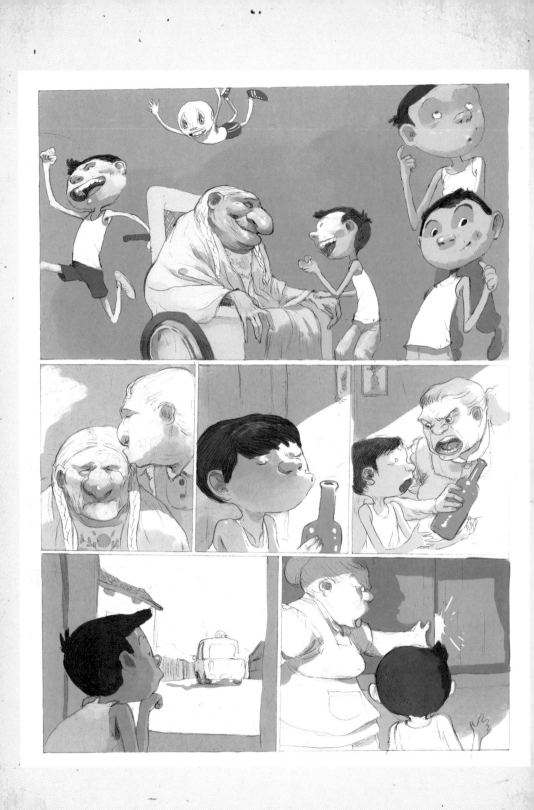